D1711029

I dedicate this entire series to anybody out there who has ever had a dream that they've been told NO to.   Believe in yourself even when you don't believe in yourself.

KSherrie

#SODCP #MMDR

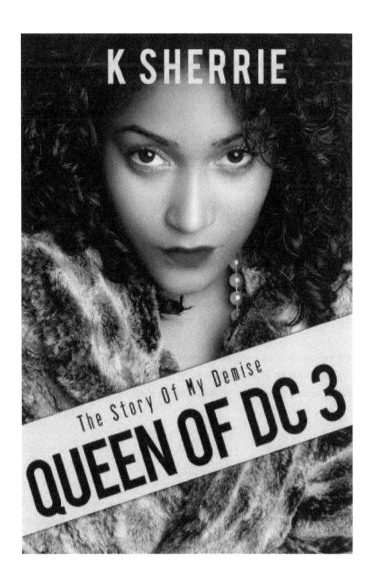

Prologue

"*This was truly the best Christmas ever. Me and Juan were gonna get married and spend forever together. I couldn't ask for anything more in this life. I had my health, an amazing man at my side, a BEAUTIFUL family, WEALTH beyond my wildest dreams. I was officially LIVING.*

We celebrated our engagement with the rest of the family Christmas morning over breakfast. Everybody knew Juan was planning to pop the question but me. I was so shocked to learn he had actually been nervous and was worried I might say no.

Picture that shit.

The same way he was thanking God daily for bringing me back into his life, I was giving the same thanks. I felt the kind of love for Juan that would make me trade it all just to be his girl. That foolish love.... take heed.

The minute we stepped foot back on American soil, we started making preparations for our upcoming wedding set for June 26, 2002 and for me to step down as Queen of the fucking United States and just focus on being Queen of our castle. We decided that once we were married we were gonna move out to the west coast. So we flew out there in February and settled on a 122 million dollar Ranch Estate in Santa Monica. It was located about 3 miles from the Neverland Ranch. I didn't know what our combined net worth was at the time but I knew we had to be sitting on a shitload of shoeboxes to be able to kick it in Michael Jackson Neighborhood.

Life was Fan-fucking-tastic!

After we closed on our home out west, I approached Ciaira about buying QDC. She informed me that their businesses were doing way better than predicted and they were ready to wash their hands with the street also. The Queen and the Princess were stepping out of the kingdom together. Now I needed another buyer so I went to my second right hand.

CoCo.

CoCo had a lot of years invested in the organization. She was there for me when the bitches I originally jumped off the porch with wasn't. She was family by more than just blood. By hustle, by loyalty. She worked directly at my side for so long I felt she was right to be my successor.... second choice yes, but a choice none the less. Ty crossed my mind also but I wanted another Queen to step into my shoes. I had mad love for Ty. He was family and he would've been my next choice not because he wasn't good enough for first pick BUT because it was enough niggas in the world calling the shots.... I kicked in the door laying motherfuckas down so me and my girls would have a chance. I wanted us to continue to rise as woman. Fuck being "That nigga wifey... bitch BE THAT NIGGA." was what we used to say back in the day. CoCo jumped on the opportunity before the words settled good in the air. I knew my girl aint have the 2 billion I wanted out the gate so I put her on a payment plan. We worked out a plan that had me giving her them thangs for a measly ass 10 grand a piece, then she was to pay me 25 million dollars per month towards ownership of the business. This would be our layout for the next 7 year then she would officially be Queen. Right now her ass was just acting.

I didn't see it at the time because I was so busy riding my high horse. Being in love and shit, raising my family, building a successful business portfolio, taking exotic vacations and shit, planning to get married and whipping my ass with thousand dollar bills. But apparently according to the laws of physics, what goes up MUST come down. The Sun and the moon included. Well my starry eyed ass had apparently been UP for far too long. Motherfuckas aint gonna be too keen to see a bitch living swell forever.

Word to Lemony Snickets, leaving my cousin's home with a deal signed in the sense of a handshake, I had no idea the series of unfortunate events that were getting ready to unfold in my life and bring everything full circle. Sometimes where you start is right where you finish in this world. And the people you trust the most can and will be your own undoing."

"Family Issues"

June 2003

"Everything was truly everything in my world these days. Me and Juan were in love like never before. Every morning when I woke up, I stopped, dropped to my knees and thanked GOD for this man in my life. To say we were blessed was a gross understatement. We had a house full of healthy, happy, spoiled kids. We were owners of a number of profitable businesses. We were billionaires and our fairytale one of a kind wedding was approaching extremely fast. I was beyond thankful for our wedding planner. When we met with her and decided that she was the one, Juan put a briefcase in her hands with 2 million dollars cash inside to let her know that money was no object and whatever I wanted this wedding to be..... she needed to make it happen. So many women have told me, including the wedding planner and even my mother that their weddings had been planned out in their heads from before they even had tiddies good. Only thing they needed was the groom. Me...... I never thought about or pictured myself standing anywhere in anybody wedding dress UNTIL I met Juan. Even then, I thought about and fanaticized about being his WIFE. The wedding scene just wasnt my thing. The wedding planner started shooting her visions and I knew the minute she started talking I had to be hands on with this shit. I wanted a wedding that represented US, and who we were... that was 100 % original.

Before Juan removed himself from the wedding planning because he said it was "Woman's work" we decided on a location. We went back and forth and finally decided to do Key West Florida. It was exotic but still within the lower 48 so nobody would be left out.

From January 3rd 2002 til June 1st 2003 me and the wedding planner met twice a week to touch basis on the beautiful exotic Oceanside wedding. We were originally planning to marry that same year but needed a little more time to do what we wanted how we wanted. But it was all good, it just gave us another year to grow together and love harder. We decided to Honeymoon in South Africa for a Month. By June 1st, everything was paid for, booked and ready for our big day.

We invited 400 people to our wedding and paid for everything. We were shutting Key West Down that weekend and I couldn't wait. On June 10, me and Juan along with out immediate family, the entire wedding party, the planner and her crew of 6 flew to Miami, where we all would be staying and then carting off to Key West for the actual ceremony. Everyone else.... the guest, the photographers and videographers, and entertainment for the reception and such was arriving on the 15th.

I had been enjoying our time in paradise and excitedly, yet nervously counting down the days until I married the man of my dreams. It was still surreal to me. I constantly thought back to the days of only longing to tell Juan how much I loved him, or witness the smile that served to brighten my day…. and now here I was getting ready for a couple of forevers with him.

As our guest started funneling in, and the final I's were dotted and T's crossed I breathed a sigh of relief. I had gotten accustomed to drama invading my space and trying it's damndest to turn my smiles upside down…. but this time around, everything was good. All I had to do now was make it through 2 more days and my true fairytale would be beginning…… You think I would have learned by now to stop counting my blessings before I saw them through.

Woe Is Me.

I wanted to be available to see all my guest as they made their way into paradise to help us celebrate our grand occasion, but preparing to become Juan's wife was not an easy task by far so I found myself busy as hell managing the manager of my wedding. Everything had to be perfect down to the last grain of rice. I mean, this is Juan and Keeli's wedding ya know.

We finally made it down to the wire and had our rehearsal dinner. We went down to Key West to the Mansion the wedding would take place in, had the rehearsal, and then came all the way back to Miami for the dinner. When the pastor said his final prayer and we all got ready to leave, I was so excited to know we were just about at the finish line.... well starting line to our new life together as husband and wife.

Although I was stoked about being an arms length from my wedding day, I was also excited to know my family was IN THE MOTHERFUCKIN BUILDING. The whole QDC fam was in Miami for the festivities. And I couldn't wait to see them. Living up in New York and being a legit business woman didn't leave much time for me to kick it with my peoples and I missed them. My family by blood and my family by hustle. I had decided earlier in the day that I was gonna get up with them after the rehearsal dinner..... but of course my HUSBAND TO BE had plans of his own."

Keeli and Juan are exiting the restaurant after their rehearsal dinner arm in arm surrounded by their family and wedding party. Juan playfully squeezes Keeli's nipple when he thinks no one is looking and she giggles like a school girl. "My father said he taking the boys tonight and my mother got the girls so you already know what that means"

"Do I really?" Keeli blushes.

"Hell yeah, I get me one more night of sin filled fornication with the woman of my dreams." Juan says seductively.

"That sounds like fun. So I will meet you back at our room at......"

"Meet me?" Juan pulls away from Keeli. "Where the hell you going?"

"I thought I told you, me and Ciaira gonna swing pass the hotel and see our peoples. Have a quick drink and such with them."

"Come on Ke...." Juan begins to protest. "You will see all them bitches at the bridal shower tomorrow night."

"Babe relax. Just give me like 2 hours tops and I'm back, butt naked showing off my lack of gag reflexes." Keeli laughs.

Juan smiles, now pleased with her plans. "Just hurry up man. Take too long and I'ma have to punish that ass LITERALLY."

"Whatever." Keeli kisses him softly on the lips and then signals for Ciaira to come on.

"It was hard as hell to pull myself away from that man that night.... but it was true that absence makes the heart grow fonder and the dick get harder so although I SAID two hours, I HAD to stay gone at minimum 3 hours to get that "I want you soo bad but you so fucking hard headed you gotta be taught a lesson" dick..... that was the kinda shit that made your write home to mama I swear.

Me and Ciaira hopped in the back of one of the chauffeured Navigators we had access to during our stay and headed across town to the resort my guest was staying at. I was surprised as hell to find out that only my street family was NOT staying there. Now I knew my peoples were IN Miami, it was just a matter of where at. So I did some quick calling and searching and found my crew...... waaaay on the other side of town in a fucking Ramada Limited of all places. I was feeling 8 kinds of ways as we rolled up on this shit. When we walked into the lobby, we immediately started seeing that QDC family deep. The hotel was Shabby as shit, but they was making the most out of it. After we said what's up to a few folks in the lobby, we made our way out to the pool area where we came upon Donna and the crew. I was really feeling some kinda way seeing the shabby ass dibs my people had been put up in and wasn't truly understanding why.... but I was damn sure gonna find out. I ordered a round of drinks from the poolside bar for everybody out there..... even the folks I didn't know because well.... fuck we needed to be drunk to be in this motherfucka. After the hugs and what's up and a quick toast to family, something dawned on me...... I didn't even see my OWN family in the building. It was time to get to the bottom of whatever the fuck was afoot."

Keeli turns to Jesse who is standing next to her and ask the million dollar question. "Hold up y'all where CoCo and Tiff at?"

"Maaaan, don't nobody out here fuck with them bitches."

"Whoa Whoa, I know you better watch your motherfuckin mouth. That's FAMILY you speaking on."

"No disrespect Ke, But aint nobody fucking with them chicks for real. It is what it is." Jesse refuse to back down from her initial stance.

"For real, for real Ke, you need to stop boo loving and get back like yesterday." Donna adds while shaking her head in disgust from just thinking about the situation.

"What the fuck is going on yo?" Ciaira asks in confusion.

"It's real simple, Y'all peoples on some other shit these days." Shameka adds then sips her drink.

Just then Ty walks up behind Keeli and covers her eyes playfully and whispers in her ear. "Guess who nigga."

"TY!!" Keeli screams with delight as she turns and hugs him tight. "What's happening baby! Nigga I miss yo ass!"

"I miss you too boo. But aint nothing. Same ole shit, different day."

Keeli shoves Ty in his chest. "I'm mad at your ass anyway. You can't never pick up the phone and call me. Nigga you my brother. How you gonna do me like that."

"How was I gonna call you Ke? I aint got your digits?"

"Why not? I gave my new numbers to CoCo to give to everybody."

"Maaaaan fuck them bitches yo." Ty says as he spits on the ground as if disgusted with just hearing CoCo's name.

"Man what the fuck is wrong with y'all? Y'all motherfuckas spitting real greasy about my peoples like I aint standing here. THE FUCK. Don't bite the motherfuckin hand that feed you yo."

"Feed who?" Donna interjects "Don't none of us work for or do no kinds of business with them broads."

"Man what the fuck is REALLY going on in this house?" Ciaira asks.

"And fuck y'all keep saying THEM for? My sister aint got shit to do with shit." Ty starts laughing in disbelief. "Ooooh so you really don't know."

"KNOW WHAT!" Keeli snaps.

"I really think we need to sit down and rap a taste Keeli." Shameka says.

"You would be surprised at what's really good in the hood these days."

"Come on, let's go to my room." Ty suggest.

The girls get up and they all follow Ty back inside the hotel and get on the elevator. No words are spoken as they travel to the 4th floor and get off and walk down the hall and into Ty's room. As soon as Ty locks the door, Keeli breaks her silence. "Now what the fuck is going on yo."

"Where do we even begin." Donna giggles.

"At the motherfuckin beginning." Keeli snaps.

"Well for starters, aint no QDC INC no more. We all got out cause your peoples are truly on some other shit." Shameka says.

"Since you sold the company to CoCo, this bitch been on some other shit. Straight power tripping. And your dumb ass sister right along with her. I walked away back in February." Ty says.

"And we all officially broke out back in April." Jesse adds.

"See the power tripping wasn't my issue... I could've dealt with that." Ty begins. "But when they shitted on my whole squad, I had to throw in my towel."

"What you mean?" Keeli asks confused.

"My folks up in Ohio, They sold them people 25 bricks of bullshit and 25 bricks of fucking cement. I had to pay them people back out my own pockets." Keeli and Ciaira both sit there with their mouths hanging open in disbelief of what they are hearing. "Then this bitch talking about my man lying. He playing games. Now how the fuck that sound Keeli? My peoples dealt with you for almost 5 years straight. No funny business. Nigga sitting on MILLIONS thanks to this organization. So why would he wanna play dirty now?"

"I feel you Ty." Ciaira says still shocked by the news they are receiving.

"And we handed in our walking papers when they bitches started up that bullshit with Daye." Donna starts.

"What shit?" Keeli asks, rubbing her temples as the stress begins to seep in.

"They got some niggas to rob one of his spots. They took like 300 G's and 4 keys AND Kidnapped the nigga baby mother and tried to get a fucking ransom from this man. Word is, he was like Kill that bitch then cause I aint paying.... assuming these motherfuckas knew better. But they didn't."

"They killed her and left her body down on the field for them to find." Shameka adds.

"Oh my God. Please tell me y'all fucking lying."

"I wish we was. For like 2 weeks after that we couldn't be on the block. They was just like aint no work"

"And them bitches aint even attempt to pay us like you always did Keeli." Jesse adds.

"But I'm walking my kids to school one morning and I get approached by Daye's peoples. They say they bringing word straight from Jake B." Donna continues with her story.

"The Jamaican dude?" Keeli asks, now even more confused. "What the fuck he got to do with anything?"

"Word was, if me and my peoples don't wanna die, he suggest we stop fucking with these QDC bitches IMMEDIATELY."

"It's a fucking bounty on all 4 of their heads Keeli. A million dollars a piece." Shameka adds. "So don't be surprised if a motherfucka try and knock their shit loose right after your wedding. Not saying it would be none of us, but you got virtually the whole fucking city down here and EVERYBODY knows about that bounty."

"Trust me, them getting hit at my wedding is the least of my worries. If that shit attempted to happen, they wouldn't get off the grounds alive. Just trust me on that.

"Yeah, I hear them in-laws got reach." Ty adds.

"That's neither here not there. What the fuck does Jake B have to do with any of this. Why is this shit with Daye even his concern?" Ciaira asks.

"Y'all remember Netta right?" Donna asks

"Yeah." Keeli and Ciaira reply in unison.

"Well she fuck with one of Daye peoples, and from what she told us is the broad they killed was Jake B's daughter. And the dope and money they snatched all had his name on it."

"Wait a minute. Go back a second. Y'all sad it's a bounty on all 4 of them..... what 4?"

"The dudes!" Shameka adds.

"Oh y'all aint know about the two clown ass niggas they got holding them down?" Jesse laughs.

"Right! Now listen to this shit Keeli." Ty begins. "When I left I went to CoCo cause you know me and her always been cool. So I'm like look sis, even though I aint working with y'all nomore and y'all done shitted on my family.... cut all of 46 loose...."

"They did what!" Keeli yells in shock.

"Yeah they cut the whole squad loose. Told them fuck y'all in a sense."

"That was Tiff idea." Shameka adds. "She was like can't none of them niggas eat nomore cause they fuck with Ty. And niggas who shake his hand starve in her world."

"See the stupid shit I'm talking about?" Ty ask while shaking his head in disbelief and then continues with his story. " But since I had spent damn near all my funds paying them Ohio niggas back, I go to CoCo and I'm like look, I got 50.... let get get 3 of them thangs at the family rate. Her man steps up and he like AINT NO FAMILY RATE HOMEY. So I'm like ok OG, we'll drop me a line on your supplier and he talking about I AM THE SUPPLIER. I knew that was bullshit but I wasn't about to beg this random nigga, hat in hand so I took my money elsewhere. I got with my man from the islands and he plugged me in with his man and I got me 5 pounds. So me and Spyda been working that to keep eating."

"You selling weed now?" Keeli asks in disgust.

"Nigga's gotta eat baby."

"If this nigga selling weed these days.... what the fuck is y'all doing?" Ciaira asks while pointing at the girls, actually kinda scared of what their hustle might be.

"Me and Meka pulled our lil money together and got a lil salon down H Street." Donna says.

"Man what room them bitches in?" Keeli snaps.

Shameka laughs. "Oh them bitches aint here. They staying at the big house. They over at that swanky ass resort playing in the big pool."

"No they not. We got a list of all the resort guest and they aint on it so they gotta be here with y'all."

"I'm telling you they not Ke. If them price tagged hoes was here. Trust me we wouldn't be."

"How the fuck y'all end up here in this shabby ass place anyway?" Keeli enquires.

"Cause when we got to the airport and seen we was gonna be on the same plane with them bitches we all said fuck that shit. Jake B the type of motherfucka that will blow up a whole plane to get at one person..... wasn't no fucking way we was stepping on a plane with them hoes. So we all took a later flight."

"When we arrived late, the wedding planner chick brought us here."

"Man, go pack y'all shit." Keeli demands. "Round up the whole crew and tell them get their shit. Let's bounce."
"Where we going?" Shameka enquires.
"Not here for sure. Bitch got my family fucked up."

"I whipped out my cell and called Sharon the wedding planner/coordinator quick and let her ass HAVE IT. She was trying hard to explain how my folks ended up in the Ramada Limited but I wasn't hearing it. I told her she had exactly 30 minutes to get 25 rooms and personally escort my fucking folks to them. Then I asked the million dollar question.... where the fuck was my cousin and sister. When she told me, I almost lost it.

So the rooms at The Palms I was springing for wasn't good enough for these two bitches. Apparently THEY let Sharon have it and demanded to be moved Mandarin Oriental.... The Presidential Suite. I did not speak another word... just hung up the phone and headed for the door. I needed to check these ho's ASAP cause apparently they had life fucked up. But I was gonna fix it no doubt. Once we got into the Navigator, I shot Sharon a text telling her let me know the minute she got my people situated and then rode across town in silence.

We pulled up to the Hotel and my heels were clicking across the pavement before the truck even stopped completely. Ciaira had to run to keep up with me. I stormed through the lobby and straight to the elevator.... there was no access to the Penthouses from there. As soon as I stepped out I saw a sign telling me which way the penthouse elevators were. I started off towards them and then saw you needed a penthouse key to even access that elevator. I walked over to the front desk, trying hard as hell to stifle the explosion in me but no haps. I was ready to blow and the dumb ass front desk chick was the unfortunate receiver of my wrath."

"Good Evening. Welcome to Mandarin Oriental Miami." The front desk agent greets with a smile. "How may I assist you this evening."

"I need go to the presidential suite NOW." Keeli snaps.

"I'm sorry ma'am. Only our guest who are occupying the presidential suite and their approve guest have access to those floors. May I ask what the guest you wish to see names are?"

"Katherine Byrd and Tiffany Cole." Keeli snaps again on the verge of losing her cool.

"I can call ahead and see if they will allow you up ma'am."

"Allow me up?? Bitch do you know who the fuck I am??" Keeli snaps at the unsuspecting clerk. "Bitch you better check the fucking card on file to pay for that shit and give me the fucking key to get up there before you have a motherfucking problem on your hand your ditsy bleach blonde ass aint prepared to fucking deal with!!"

"Yo Ke, chill man." Ciaira tries to calm Keeli down as she realizes the entire buzzing lobby had come to a screeching halt and were focused on them. The desk clerk runs away from the counter crying into the back and the Guest Manager comes to the counter.

"Ma'am, is there a problem of some sort?" The guest manager enquires.

"Hell yeah there is a problem." Keeli snaps at him.

"Chill man." Ciaira says as she steps in front of Keeli to speak with the guest manager. "Good evening, I do apologize for my sister's outburst."

"Don't be fucking apologizing for me!"

"My sister just received notice that her credit card is being used to pay for a room for two of her wedding guest here at your hotel without her permission.... and it's not just any room, it's y'all presidential suite."

"I do apologize ma'am." The guest Manager starts typing into the computer. "What are the guest names ma'am?"

"Katherine Byrd and Tiffany Cole."

"And your name ma'am?"

"Keeli Byrd." Ciaira answers for her. "The card was authorized by the wedding planner Sharon Miller of Miller Events."

"I see. Again I do apologize whole heartedly for our staff and any upsets this may have caused you. I will have security escort them out immediately."

"That wont be necessary." Keeli interrupts. "I'll eat the bill for tonight. Just take me to their room."

"Immediately ma'am. Just let me grab the elevator key and I will personally escort you up."

"Thank You."

The guest clerk pulls a key card from the drawer and leads the girls over to the private elevator. They take it up to the 20th floor.

"I was past upset at this point. I was downright ANGRY. Who the fuck did these bitches think they were?? Everybody on every one of my blocks worked their asses off. No Slackers. And for these two sluts to shit on my people was like shitting on me and y'all already KNOW I wasn't going for that by any stretch of the imagination. They out here giving the shit I built from the ground up a bad rep with their bullshit. As long as I have been in this

business, I aint NEVER do people dirty. I played fair with everybody so what the fuck was these ho's tryna do? Then I really wasn't understanding this shit with Daye. Why the fuck were they fucking with this man?

Since 1996, me and this man ran shops LITERALLY right around the corner from each other and never had a problem. No robbing, no killing, no beefing. Shit we was like ghost to each other. We never said a word to each other... but we respected each others hustle. Now these bitches done been on the scene a year and managed to get a whole fucking BOUNTY on their head.

Then to top this shit off, these bitches was ruining my big day. They got me on a private fucking elevator asking permission to come up and beg their fucking pardon. You could see the smoke coming out of my ears. I was truly not feeling these bitches AT ALL.

I don't know if this was normal speed but the elevator ride seemed to take forever. The poor Guest Manager looked petrified. I didn't plan on taking my anger out on him as long as he continued to lead me to the spot where dumb bitches dwell."

The elevator dings and the doors open. Keeli and Ciaira step off as the Guest Manager holds the door for them. "Thank you. We will have out guest bring us down." Ciaira informs him.

"Not a problem. Please don't hesitate to let me know if you ladies need anything else."

"Thank You." Keeli says and heads towards the large doors at the end of the hall indicating their conversation is over. Ciaira speed walks to catch up with her. "I'm putting their asses out tonight."

"Really Ke?"

"Fuck yeah. I don't even wanna know how much this fucking room cross. A whole private floor tho Ciaira. These bitches tripping."

"Just be calm boo. I know you not tryna find your ass sitting in the slammer two days before your wedding."

"Ci, I bullshit you not. I am as calm as I'ma get." Keeli says as she rings the doorbell. The girls stand and wait a whole two minutes and then Keeli starts to bang on the door with her fist. After another minute goes by and she begins to kick the door. Ciaira stops her while cracking up laughing. "What the fuck you laughing for yo!" Keeli snaps,

"Chill boo. You know it's hard as fuck to hear in these big ass rooms."

"Bitch you aint funny." Keeli can't help but laugh.

"Then why you laughing." Ciaira asks, happy to have calmed her best friend down enough to get her to laugh.

Just then, Tiffany opens the door in a short red silk bathrobe. "Hey Boo! Look at you looking all fly and shit! Come on in!"

Keeli and Ciaira walk into the Suite and Tiffany closes the door. The girls stand in the foyer and take in the living room area of the suite and the mess it has become. There are clothes, shoes, Liquor bottles, blunt trash, cigarette butts, leftover food and just stuff everywhere. Keeli walks over to the large sectional sofa and pushes everything on the floor and sits down. Ciaira sits down beside her and Tiffany flops down on the Love Seat.

"So you ready for your big day sis?"

"Yep."

"Yo I still can't believe you and this nigga getting married. I still remember the first time I met him. That night you and him was fighting at his crib and shit. Now y'all bout to get married. That shit crazy."

"Yeah, anyway what's up? Where CoCo at?"

"Oh, she went down to curse out the motherfucking room service staff." Tiffany boast proudly.

"Why?" Ciaira asks barely able to hold in her laughter.

"Girl we ordered lobster for dinner and hers was small as shit and she wasn't having it."

"How long she been gone because I need to holla at both of y'all like right now?"

"They should be on their way up now. I'll be right back, I gotta go to the bathroom." Tiffany excuses herself and leaves the living room area and goes down the hall into one of the bathrooms. Ciaira gets up and begins to walk around the disgusting room. She walks into the dining room area and stops dead in her tracks. "Ke, come here quick. Look at this shit." Keeli gets up and goes into the dining room behind Ciaira. Ciaira points to the mirror on the table with coke residue on it. Keeli picks it up and shakes her head in disbelief.

"So these bitches up in here getting fucking zooted."

"Tiff ass cooked right now. You aint see her fucking eyes?"

"You know how you see shit, but you really aint tryna see that shit. Yeah that's where we at with it."

"So what you gonna do about this?"

"First I'ma wait for the motherfucking H.N.I.C to get back from stunting downstairs. Then I'ma lay down the motherfuckin law in this bitch about EVERYTHING.

"But baby aint too much you can say to them about their fucked up business practices. You did sell them...."

"That shit aint finalized. I only got 50 tickets so far on the whole deal. Bitch can get that shit back TONIGHT."

Just then CoCo and Duck come into the suite and CoCo is still reeling from the lobster incident. "And my shit better be hot when they fucking bring it back! They got me fucked up down this bitch!"

"Chill Mami them motherfuckas got your word." Duck offers further inflating CoCo's swollen ego.

"They better or Miami aint gonna be the motherfuckin same nomore." CoCo stops dead in her tracks when she sees Keeli and Ciaira standing there looking at her. "Awww shit! There go my motherfuckin peoples!" CoCo runs over and hugs the girls tight. "What's crackin baby! I thought we wouldn't see your ass until tomorrow. Oh Shit, I'm being rude. Keeli, Ciaira, this my Fiance brother Duck. Duck, this my baby Keeli and her right hand Ciaira." Duck smiles at the girls. "What's cracking ladies."

"Aint shit." Keeli snaps. Look, I need to holla at you and Tiff like RIGHT NOW."

"Ok boo, calm down. Let me go find her ass."

"She in the bathroom." Keeli informs CoCo.

"Ok, I'ma go get her. Duck can you give us a minute?"

"No problem. I'ma go hit the hot tub and relax some of these muscles." Duck walks off down the hall and CoCo is still standing in front of Keeli and Ciaira smiling for no reason. Keeli and Ciaira are looking at each other in disbelief.

"What you need something? You don't know where the bathroom at?" Keeli snaps.

"Huh?" CoCo asks in a confused tone.

"Tiffany. You were supposed to go get her so we can talk." Ciaira reminds her while shaking her head.

"Oh yeah. My bad. I'll be right back." CoCo goes down the hall and into the same bathroom Tiffany went in earlier. Keeli walks back over to the sofa and sits down shaking her head in complete disbelief.

"I honestly don't know if I was more angry or more hurt by the shit I was witnessing from these two. This was CoCo.... my second in command and Tiffany... My fucking sister. Just thinking about them two coked up bitches had me HOT. My blood was boiling fucking with these hoes. Both of them looked a complete fucking mess. These was not the same bitches I held under my wing for years. Then this dope fiend ass broad talking about her Fiancé'. Fiancé' MY ASS. These niggas was chasing money and I bet her ass was passing it out hand over fucking fist. Just a stupid ass bitch. Another thing that was fucking with me was this brother of her so called fiancé'. It was something familiar about this nigga. TOO FAMILIAR. The way this nigga smiled at me and Ciaira wasn't sitting right with me. I knew I knew this nigga from somewhere BUT I guess my anger wasn't allowing me to properly categorize him because I kept drawing a blank.... but I knew that I knew his ass from somewhere.

Me and Ciaira sat there in complete silence for 10 minutes that felt like a lifetime..... just waiting on these bitches like I was truly on their fucking time. Then, just as my patience level was approaching the somebody MUST DIE mark and I was gonna find myself in the bathroom beating the dog shit out of both these soon to be straight shooter...... the THREE of them came waltzing out of the bathroom and we had a whooooooole new can of bullshit to deal with."

A smile a mile wide crosses Jackie's face as he closes the space between him, Keeli and Ciaira. He gets within arm's length of them and extends his arms expecting a warm hug. "What's happening Love!" Keeli sits there with her mouth hanging wide open and her heart racing a mile a minute. "Dammmmn, y'all don't even know a nigga no more huh. No Luv at all."

"Wait.... You know them?" Tiffany enquires.

"Oh hell yeah." Jackie chuckles. He walks over and sits beside Keeli on the sofa and puts his arm around her. "This here was wifey. My fucking heart!"

"Damn. I guess this is a small world afterall." CoCo says.

"It sure is." Jackie agrees.

"How fucking long you been home?" Ciaira asks. "I really can't believe you sitting here yo."

" I been home a minute. Close to a year now."

"And how the fuck did you get out? I was in the courtroom on sentencing day nigga." Ciaira asks.

"I know. But you would be surprised what knowing the right people....."

"And having a couple million dollars will get you." Tiffany finishes for him. Keeli stands up and starts to walk across the room towards the foyer and front door. "Yo Ke, where you going baby?" Jackie asks while smiling. Keeli walks out the door. Ciaira gets up and goes behind her. She catches up with Keeli at the elevator. "Come on Ke.... you gotta say something."

"I gotta get the fuck outta here."

"How we gonna get downstairs? You need the keycard for the elevator."

"Please go get it. I gotta get the fuck away from here NOW!"

"Ok. Just calm down. I'll be right back." Ciaira goes back down the hall into the suite. Keeli leans against the wall and shakes her head in disgust and disbelief. She chuckles at the situation.... not ha ha this shit is funny chuckle, more of I can't fucking believe this chuckle. Ciaira comes back out of the suite followed by Tiffany and CoCo. They all come down to the elevator.

"You alright?" CoCo asks with concern.

"Yeah. Just let me on the elevator yo."

26

CoCo swipes the keycard and the elevator starts making the trek up from the lobby. Tiffany looks at her sister through narrow, malice filled eyes. "So you and Jackie used to mess with each other huh.?"

Keeli chuckles and shakes her head. "Yeah Tiff, you can say that I guess."

"This must be real awkward for you then." CoCo adds.

"Like you wouldn't believe."

"So was y'all serious or what?" Tiffany asks with her tone laced with attitude.

"What?" Keeli asks dumbfounded and Ciaria begins to crack up laughing.

"On a scale of 1 to 10, how serious would you say y'all was? Tiffany demands to know.

The elevator arrives and Keeli and Ciaira step on it. Keeli holds the doors open by pressing the button. "All this bullshit aside, I need to meet with y'all in the morning."

"Ok. When?" CoCo inquires.

"I'll call. Just be ready. I'll send a car to pick THE TWO OF YOU up. Hear me good, THE TWO OF YOU."

"Ok."

Keeli lets go of the button and the doors begin to close. Tiffany sticks her foot in the door to stop the doors from closing. "You still didn't answer my question." Tiffany snaps, not even pretending to hide her attitude. "I wanna know how serious you and Jackie was."

"You really wanna know?" Keeli laughs.

"Yes I do!"

"He's CiCi's fucking father!"

Tiffany and CoCo both stand in in silence with their mouths hanging open as the elevator doors close and Keeli and Ciaira head to the lobby.

"If there was any doubt in my mind who Jackie was here with, my little sister and her fucking attitude and questioning of me like I wouldn't knock her fucking teeth

down her throat had immediately cleared that shit up. This nigga being here.... in my life in ANY form, in my space, breathing my free motherfuckin air was the very last thing I expected to encounter when I woke up this morning. Now I needed to know what the hell his motive was. Everybody on this planet has one, Him..... You..... ME. And anybody who tries to convince you they don't.... get the fuck away from them QUICK. Cause they lying.

Me and Ciaira made it back to the truck and got in but we rode in complete silence. What part of the game was this was all I was trying to figure out. Of all the chicks on earth, this nigga shows up with my sister. And more importantly FREE. Like Ciaira said we were IN the fucking courtroom so I was truly not understanding this fluke shit.

And two fucking days before the biggest day of my life. Yeah it was definitely some ole bullshit in the pot disguised as soup.

Now I hope you aint looking at these pages and thinking a bitch was jealous or no bullshit like that cause you should know by now that Keeli don't get jealous. But something about this whole situation made me uneasy as fuck. I decided that when I got back to the room, I was gonna call downstairs and see if they could get me a chess set. Since Simm first put me on to that shit, it was how I dealt. How I calmed myself. I was positive I wouldn't have made it this far in this cut throat game had it not been for chess. But the minute I stepped off the elevator and made it to the duplex penthouse suite of Marenas, where we were staying.... I quickly realized the Husband to be had plans of his own that in no way included a chess board or the bullshit from my previous life.

When I stepped through the door, I was reminded of why I loved this man so much. The sent of Vanilla engulfed me. He had candles lit and placed all along the first level of our suite. My favorite smell of Vanilla was having a battle with my second favorite smell..... FRESH ROSES. There were about 20 dozen placed all around in some of the most beautiful vases I had ever seen. There were white roses which were my favorite, red, pink and yellow and one vase filled with blue roses. I walked through the first level blushing like a fool. It was amazing to me how a man of Juan's stature held so much romance and love for me in his heart. As much shit I had done in my life, I know deep inside I didn't deserve the kind of love this man showered me with daily.... I mean truthfully speaking I was fucked up. I used people, I killed people, I supplied a product that made children go to bed hungry at night while mine flew in private jets and sailed on yachts. Yeah I had a real fucked up streak about me, but God saw favor in me and brought me the kind of love most bitches only dream about.

I stood there listening to Luther Vandross crooning out the live version of If Only For One Night with a smile spread wide across my face. Then I spotted the large white box with the huge red bow sitting on the coffee table in the center of the living room area. Beside it was a glass of something chilled and bubbly. I loved surprises from Juan, and a few splashes always made me giddy. So I sat down and sipped and opened the card on top of the box. It simply stated "Wear this. I'm waiting."

I opened the box and inside I found nothing but a diamond necklace. I loooooved Diamonds. I couldn't stop smiling. I was like the school girl who had just saw the basketball player she has a crush on. Juan was everything for real. I didn't want to waste any more time so I stood and began to slide out of my clothes. After I removed every stitch of fabric from my body, I let my hair down and then put on my newest trinket from Papi. It rested against my skin and seem to sparkle even brighter. I finished my drink and headed for the stairs. I caught a glimpse of myself in the hallway on one of the long mirrors and maaaaaan. I was one bad ass chick. It still amazed me at times that I was the same chick who years back had to beg and borrow on so many occasions to feed my son. Had slept on peoples living room floors too many times to count because my mother couldn't make rent too many times and we had to go. Now here I was ascending the stairs in the fucking penthouse suite of the Marenas to go and fuck my rich ass husband until his dick would stand no more. I blew myself a kiss and winked and then continued my mission.

I followed the rose petals up the winding staircase and down the hall to the huge master suite at the very end.

There were more candles and more roses that lead the way to the palace of love. I could feel my love box getting wet with anticipation of Juan's touch. I opened the double doors and there I found the man of my dreams..... all I've ever wanted... waiting for me.

The blackout drapes were pulled back and the only light was provided by the moon. The bed was covered in more rose petals, and there was my Papi. He was sitting in the chaise, smoking a nice fat blunt of loud wearing nothing but a pair of black silk boxers. I couldn't wait to get my hands on this man. Although I swear me and Juan fucked what seemed like every night.... every single time was like the first time to me. I never got tired of his love. He smiled at me and I swear my nipples felt as though they were gonna explode they got so hard. He extended the blunt to me and I made my way to him and he pulled my naked body to him and held me tight and kissed my lips like he longed for the kiss since the day he was born.

Damn I couldn't wait to be this man's wife!"

"I thought you had changed your mind for a minute." Juan jokes.
"Now picture that." Keeli chuckles. " You know you fucked up right. This some honeymoon type shit Papi."
"Nah, this gonna be some everyday type shit for us baby."
"I like the way that sound." Keeli blushes.

"I bet you do with your spoiled ass." Juan lovingly smacks Keeli's ass.

"You made me this way." Keeli takes a hard pull from the blunt as Juan begins to rub her shoulders.

"What's wrong Mami? You feel tensed."

"I am Papi. Like you wouldn't believe."

"Tell Papi what's wrong."

"It can wait. You went through all this trouble to make this nice special for us and I don't wanna ruin it by spending our time talking about this bullshit."

"Nah, you will ruin it by keeping it bottled in. Cause once we finish this L, I got some plans for you and that juice box. I want you all in.... Mind, Body and Soul. So tell me what's eating at you." Juan rubs his fingers gently against Keeli's love button. "Other than me real soon."

Keeli blushes with delight and hits the blunt again before passing it back to Juan. "Ok, so first your wedding planner pulls a major violation and throws my people in a fucking shithole hotel. So I had to bomb her ass out and make her fix it. Then I find out it's beef in my crew. CoCo and Tiff gone off the deep in, fucking with that glass."

"Are you serious boo?"

"Yes. Then these bitches decide the rooms we paid for aint good enough for them and have your dumb ass wedding planner set them up at the fucking Mandarin.... In the Presidential Suite all on our dime. And THEN...."

"It's more?"

"Hell yeah, this the cake topper baby. You ready for this shit?"

"Shit, the way you sound.... " Juan Chuckles.

"CiCi fucking father is here?"

"What?"

"Yeah. He happens to be fucking my sister these days. So the nigga is her plus one at our wedding."

"I thought that nigga had like a 100 years?"

"So did I. I can't even process this bullshit. I'm meeting with Tiff and CoCo in the morning and I'ma let them bitches have it and then them and their boy can find their asses on the first thing smoking back to DC."

Juan puts the blunt out in the ashtray and begins to softly kiss Keeli's neck while he slides one hand between her legs and begins to teasingly rub her clit, while his other hand begins to command the attention of her nipples. Keeli lays back into him as she slides her legs open to give him full access to her love and moans with delight at the feelings he's giving her. "Let that shit go baby. This time is about us. If they wanna fuck with that glass, let them. They wanna fake stunt in the presidential suite, that shit aint about nothing. Lil sis wanna fuck with your past... Let her have it. Them bitches can't fuck with you by any stretch of the imagination. You a fucking Billionaire Keeli. A Boss baby. Stop tripping like a hourly employee. You feel me baby?"
"Yes Papi." Keeli moans as she takes in the knowledge Juan is kicking.
"Now I want you to lay back, relax, and let me knock the lining out that pussy tonight."
Keeli stands up and grabs Juan by his hands and pulls him up and can't help but smile at his large dick greeting her through the slit in his boxers.

"I lead my husband to be over to the bed and climbed atop that big motherfucka and gently helped free him and that mile o' dick he toted around from the fabric made prison known as his boxers and then I began to bless him with his favorite treat..... "dirty bitch in an alley" head. It was my way of saying thank you for all that he had done for me.... not just tonight but over the years. For finding me worthy of baring his children and wearing his name. My nasty girl head was just the beginning of our "should've made a sex tape" night. We went hard in the paint for real that night. In hindsight I was thankful the kids were out because man.... all those sounds of the jungle would've fucked them babies up for life. My head game had set the tone and we ended up going straight barbaric up in that bitch.

I don't remember what time it happened, but somewhere in the wee hours of the morning after we both were completely spent... meaning we couldn't cum again if it was money on the table, we passed out and slept like a fucking King and Queen. We were awakened at 7:30 in the morning. Infiniti had arranged to have breakfast delivered to us. It was a gift from all the kids. Juan was pissed that our sleep had been disturbed but just like I, realized we had some pretty awesome children. They genuinely loved and cared about us. After Juan let them in and they set up breakfast for us, we went into the bathroom to wash away last night. Just a quick tidy up and then we found solace in the comfort of our robes and made it downstairs to the kitchen to indulge in our last breakfast together as fornicators."

After Keeli pops two tylenol and downs her glass of orange juice to combat her slight hangover, she blows Juan a kiss across the table and he smiles at her.

"How you feeling this morning future wife?"

"I feel amazing Papi. Thank you for last night."

"No need to thank me. But I'm glad you feeling better. You was stressing last night."

"I still am in a way baby."

"So you not gonna listen to what I said?" Juan asks with his tone becoming more serious.

"Baby, you know I truly value your opinion and I always listen to your game plan. But this time I gotta call an audible and run my

own play. What I told you last night is only the half of the fuck shit these bitches out here doing. They not only shitting on my name, they shitting on my people. You know my love for my street family runs just as deep and wide as my blood family. I hope you understand."

"You really do fuck with them folks huh."

"Like you wouldn't believe. We done been through some shit together. I can't just hang them out to dry."

"I respect your decision. You got a good heart Mami."

"And a good shot too." Keeli winks at him.

"Ayyyyyye. You aint even got to tell me. Matter of fact, come here."

"Absolutely not. We need to focus on eating because still gotta pack, and y'all supposed to be leaving at 10."

"Man I'm the motherfucking groom. I can be late."

"And have Sissy blame me..... shiiiiittttt. Nigga your ass will be down in that lobby at 9:30 with your shit waiting." Keeli and Juan both laugh.

"Alright you got that." Juan winks at Keeli.

"I should've known better than to think my future husband was accepting defeat. After we ate, I was trying to get us all packed up and next thing I knew, he had me pinned down busting my shit wide open on top of the suitcases and all. This dude was a mess. After he was finally satisfied, we took a shower together and finished packing and as my luck would have it.... it was 10:30am when we stepped off the elevator into the lobby. The gang was all there. I tried not to blush but the minute they started cracking on us I

couldn't help it. Juan wanted what he wanted and GOT what he wanted. It was that simple."

"Nigga do you NOT understand 10` o clock? Serious Unk." Juan's nephew Teddy starts in on him.

"Man shut the fuck up. I'm here now."

Sissy walks up to Keeli and gives her a stern look of disapproval. She begins to speak and her Jamaican accent is thick indicating her annoyance at the moment. " So ya let'n CiCi and doze boys go to dat dere partay with them tonight I ere."

"I'm not letting them do anything. Your son decided he was taking them."

"Y'all need to stop tripping. These little niggas done seen ass before you know." Roc adds.

"Look can y'all have this conversation later, we got places to be." Juan's cousin Rico interrupts eager to get the festivities on the way.

"Alright. We will see y'all ladies in the A.M" Juan smiles at them.

"Nah, y'all will see us tonight when we bust up in that motherfucka." Iyonna adds with an attitude.

"And start beating down butt naked hoes." Shane adds as her and Iyonna high 5 each other.

"Nah, all y'all gonna see is security when they stop y'all asses at the gate with them choppas." Roc adds as him and all the guys start dapping each other up, serving to piss the women off.

"Alright y'all lets get a move on." Juan suggests and the guys start to file out of the lobby with their luggage to the awaiting convoy of black SUV's waiting to drive them to Key West where Juan's Bachelor Party is being held. CiCi hugs Keeli. "Alright Ma, don't party too hard tonight."

"I won't baby. I love you."

"I love you too ma." CiCi gets his suitcase and follows the guys outside to claim his seat along the debauchery convoy. Juan pulls Keeli into him and

hugs her tight. She looks up into his eyes and smiles. He kisses her softly on her forehead. "You know this your last chance to back out." Juan teases her.
"Nigga please. Nothing in the world would stop me from becoming Mrs. Moreno tomorrow."
"Cool. So I will see you at the alter."
"Look for me. I'll be the one in white."
"Man, I have to be the luckiest man on earth." Juan kisses Keeli softly on her lips. "I love you Keeli."
"I love you more." Keeli returns his soft kiss as he lets her go. He winks at her then grabs his suitcase and heads out of the lobby. Tears start to roll down Keeli face. Sissy's sister Inda hugs her and smiles. "It's ok love. Only 30 more hours and he is yours for life." Keeli blushes at the thought and wipes her eyes.
"Now that they are gone. We gotta get the spot ready for tonight." Iyonna beams with excitement.
"Ayyyyeeee." Shane and Tia start to dance with excitement about the bachlorette party.
"What time is this shindig starting?" Keeli inquires.
"Dinner is at 8 and the party starts at 9." Sissy informs her. "And since you have a tendency to get lost so fast and can't tell time to save your life." She links her arm with Keeli's. "Me and you will be Butt Buddies all day today."
"That's fine, but I have to make a run first."
"No ma'am. This is the day before your wedding. All dat bullshit has to wait."
"It's 10:30 now. Give me until 1. I promise I will be back here by 1.

"The day had come and the inevitable fisticuffs between me and Sissy had arrived or so I thought, because the bitch was crazy if she thought we were walking around arm in arm all day. So what if I got lost or was always late. Bitch wasn't my mammy. Lucky for both of us, Sharon the

wedding planner and her crew showed up at the same time as my mother and sisters. While they were all discussing what needed to be done, I grabbed Ciaira by the arm and we slipped off. I had business to take care of and nothing was stopping that. Not even my very own MONSTER -IN-LAW.

Since we had chauffered vehicles on deck, me and Ciaira hopped in the back of one of the Tahoe's that had been reserved for us and headed to my meeting with the town fools. My Range Rover was at the Hotel but being as though this shit had the potential to get ugly I opted for a driver.

We got to the Mandarin and this time, we got no resistance and bullshit at the front desk. The clerk eagerly escorted us up to the top of the world, where apparently now dope fiends sat. Ciaira had asked me 100 times if I was sure dealing with this shit the day before my wedding was really how I wanted to play it, and I assured her each and every time it was. Tomorrow was the beginning of a new chapter in life for me, and before I could open that one peacefully, I had to close this one off right, With all 3 of these silly motherfuckas understanding who the fuck they were playing with.

As we were riding up on the elevator, something else hit me in the head. The whole time I was with Jackie, he NEVER met Tiff or CoCo. So why the fuck would they be sponsoring his jailbreak. It didn't add up. Then it hit me like a ton of bricks. Where the fuck was his used to be right hand man. He was here and I could smell his ass. I didn't know how he had managed to mix himself up in my family, but I was positive he had somehow orchestrated this whole bullshit. I guess Ciaira had been placing the pieces of the puzzle together herself because she looked over at me and let me know her D.E was in the purse she was carrying if I needed it because chances are, Simm was here and I was gonna have to finally feed that nigga the slug he had been begging for since the mid 90's. I was praying it aint come to that. But deep in my heart I knew it would."

Keeli and Ciaira walk to the Penthouse door and Keeli rings the bell. 3 minutes later, Tiffany comes and opens the door looking as though she literally just woke up. "Hey y'all. What time is it?"

"Eleven." Keeli says as her and Ciaira bump past her and make their way into the large suite. Tiffany lags behind them still trying to adjust to the "early morning" intrusion.

"What you doing here so early anyway?"

"It aint early, and I need to talk to you and CoCo. Go get her."

"She still sleep." Tiffany protest.

"I don't give a fuck! Go wake her ass up!"

"Alright. Damn. You all snapping and shit early in the morning." Tiffany starts walking down the hall towards the bedrooms.

"For the last time BITCH IT AINT EARLY!!" Keeli yells behind her. Keeli turns and walks out onto the balcony and has a seat at the table. Ciaira sits down beside her.

"I have a blunt in my purse if you need to hit it to calm your nerves."

"My nerves are calm Ci."

Tiffany and CoCo come out onto the balcony. "What's going on? What y'all doing here so early?" CoCo inquires while still trying to rub sleep from her eyes.

Ciaira grabs Keeli's mouth before she can begin to curse CoCo out also about the "so early" comment. "Just have a seat y'all. She told y'all last night to be up early because a meeting was needed so why y'all acting so surprised that we here?"

"My bad." CoCo adds as she and Tiffany take seats in the other two chairs on the balcony. Ciaira finally lets go of Keeli's mouth. "So what's going on with y'all?"

"What you mean Ke?"

"I mean what the fuck y'all call yourselves doing? Shitting on my peoples. Fucking up my business clientele, creating problems with Daye of all fucking people...."

"I don't mean no disrespect Keeli but......." Tiffany interrupts her sister.

"Hold fast. This aint got shit to do with you for real for real. I was selling my shit to CoCo. I really and truly don't even know why the fuck you here."

"Because she's my right hand Keeli. Same way Ciaira is yours. I don't move without her."

"Look I don't give a fuck if she both your hands! You bitches out here making me look bad! Selling people this bullshit you passing off as my product and then to start up some bullshit with Daye of all the motherfuckas on this earth. What the fuck is that all about? I worked right next to this nigga for 8 fucking years and me and him never so much as exchanged a fucking sideways glace. You bitches been out here off my leash for what a good fucking 13, 14 months and done got a fucking bounty put on your fucking heads! What the fuck!"

Jackie and Simm, who have been sitting in the living room area listening to the entire conversation finally walk out onto the balcony. "But I don't see what any of that shit got to do with you, considering you sold them the business." Simm says while wearing a sinister grin. Keeli and Ciaira look at each other and both laugh. Not Ha Ha this is funny laugh, but more of look at this shit laugh.

"I called it last night." Ciaira adds.

"Yeah I'm slipping. I aint call it til this morning." Keeli turns her attention to Simm who she figures to be the one leading this charge against her. " Let's be clear. I was in the PROCESS of selling this bitch my business." Keeli points at CoCo. "Not Tiff, not Jackie and DEFINITELY NOT your bitch ass. And furthermore there is still the matter of damn near two BILLION dollars that need to come my way before ANY MOTHERFUCKING BODY can stake claim to shit." Keeli stands up and holds her hand out to Simm. "So unless you, or this bitch or this nigga here got that shit in your wallet to help this bitch here run me..... YOU" Keeli points her finger in Simm's face. "YOU the one that aint got shit to do with this and need to fall the fuck back before you catch some hot shit in your motherfuckin head. AND QUICK!"

"Baby Please." CoCo stands up and steps between Keeli and Simm and lovingly rubs his bare chest. "Please just let me handle this."

"Alright." Simm ice grills Keeli. " But you need to check that high class ho before I do."

"Nigga fuck you! Your broke ass here on MY motherfuckin dime."

"You know what. I aint even gonna argue with you. Eventually, you gonna get what's coming to you. Believe that bitch."

"I'll be waiting." Keeli smiles at him.

"Come on Jack, lets bounce."

Jackie and Simm walk back into the suite and CoCo closes the door. She turns around and takes a deep sigh. "Keeli listen....."

"Fuck whatever you got to say CoCo. Hear me and Hear me good. YOU THROUGH!"

"What!"

"You out. We done. Pack up your shit, take your so called team and get the fuck. "

"WAIT! I done paid 50 fucking tickets into this shit how the fuck you gonna put me out!"

"And the minute I touch down from my honeymoon, You will get every motherfucking penny of it back. Aint shit you can say to me EVER again in life."

"Why are you fucking doing this to me?" CoCo cries with angry tears rolling down her face. Tiffany stands up from the table. "I know what the fuck this is about. You jealous. You fucking jealous of me being with Jackie and her being with Simm.

Keeli and Ciaira both crack up laughing in a HA HA THIS SHIT IS DEF COMEDY JAM FUNNY laughter. " Now this is rich. "

"That's right." Tiffany continues. "After y'all left last night, they told us every fucking thing.

"Bitch you gone crazy." Keeli laughs. "Trust and believe me when I say I don't give a flying fuck about either one of them lame ass niggas in that room. "

"BULLSHIT BITCH! You want my man but he over your ho ass. So now that's why you up in here tryna take our shit!"

"That nigga truly got you gone." Keeli laughs.

"Or maybe it's that girl." Ciaira laughs and her and Keeli dap each other.

"The fuck is you talking about. Bitch I sell drugs not fucking do them!"

"Fuck outta here with that dope girl shit." Ciaira laughs harder. "Both y'all bitches DUSTED right now."

"Anyway, I got a wedding to get ready for. So when I get back I'll see you with that 50 CoCo. Come on Ci, Let's bounce."

Keeli walks back into the suite and Ciaira gets up and follows her. CoCo and Tiffany fall in line and follow Ciaira. As Keeli passes the kitchen area Jackie comes out and stands in front of her with his hands up in mock surrender. "I don't want no beef Keeli, I just wanna talk to you."

"What the fuck for?"

"I wanna talk about Jayceon." Jackie says humbly.

"Nigga please. CiCi aint thinking about your ass. You fucking nothing to him now get the fuck outta my way!"

"Bitch that's my son! I'm his father!"

"No bitch! You are his fucking sperm donor. He's with his father right now!"

42

Tiffany takes a swing at Keeli, but Ciaira catches her arm mid air and punches her in the face hard, dropping her to her knees. Tiffany grabs her nose that is bleeding perfusley. CoCo comes to her aid as she screams at the girls. "Get out! Both you bitches get the fuck out!!"
Keeli points her finger in Jackie's face and laughs. "You better learn to control your dope fiend bitches a little better. Oh and I hope y'all brought enough gwap to pay for this big stupid ass room or you might wanna get y'all shit packed cause its 11:30. See y'all back up top." Keeli blows Jackie a kiss and her and Ciaira leave out the door.

"These clown ass broads and their trainers... aka fluke ass niggas had me going this A.M. I still couldn't believe that bitch said I was jealous of them. Like did my sister know me at all? And the bad part about it was, them two couldn't see that if I said the word, I could have either of them niggas. They were Pawns and couldn't even see it.

As soon as we reached the elevator, it dawned on us we couldn't get down. Just then the elevator dinged and it was the dude we met last night, Duck. Then I remembered who this negro was. That was Simm's little brother. We got him to escort us back to the lobby.

On the ride back to my happy place, I found myself wondering what the fuck did I ever see in either of them niggas. Well more of what I saw in Jackie because with Simm, it was all about money. I had to stop myself 4 different times from instructing the driver to take us back. I wanted to just go and beat the dog shit out both them

*dumb ass bitches and then leave them to their puppet
masters.*

*One thing was clear in the midst of this confusion and
foolishness. I had to get back like YESTERDAY. I couldn't
just chill and watch my shit crash and burn like the twin
towers. I had promised Juan I was done getting my hands
dirty, but now I had no choice. I decided right then I would
deal with explaining this bullshit to him when the time
came. Right now, I had two far more important events to
deal with. My bachelorette party and most importantly,
my wedding.*

*I told Ciaira to fire up that L she was toting around, she
knew I was stressing and let me do the honors. As I took
the first pull, and let the smoke out slow, I also let out the
bullshit and problems. This was supposed to be the
happiest time of my life and I was NOT gonna let anyone
take that from me. It was time to enjoy myself. I would
deal with the clowns when I got back to the circus.*

"At Last"

"After we dropped Ciaira off at the spot to help Shane and the crew set up for the dinner and party, I went back to the hotel. I got my kids and the 5 of us went to spend some money shopping. After shopping, we went and had a late lunch. I had to spend some time with them being as though me and Juan would be in Africa for a whole month on our honeymoon. Sissy was gonna have Infiniti and Asha. My mom was keeping Ishmel and Mecca and CiCi along with Adovia, Robby and Eric were gonna be in North Carolina at Michael Jordan's Basketball Camp. I wanted to spend some time with my damn near grown first born, but he wasn't checking for me. All he wanted was to be at that bachelor party with his dad. I figured at least he got time with one of his parents.

After lunch we went back to the hotel. Infiniti helped me get ready for my big night while the kids went swimming with relatives. She wanted to come to the bachelorette party but Juan shut that shit down before she even got it out of her mouth good. So of course we had to listen to the double standard argument, but of course Juan didn't give a shit about her argument. Wasn't no way his daughter was attending this party. Hell he didn't even want me attending and I was the guest of honor.

By time I finished getting dolled up, it was 7:30. The theme of my bachlorette party was all white. I stepped out in a pair of white Gucci shorts that hugged just right and stopped about mid thigh level. I wore a white Gucci Tank and Matching Jacket along with white Gucci sandals. My accessories from my Gucci belt, to my Gucci shades to the Diamonds that adorned my body and the flower in my hair were all black. I stepped off the elevator into the lobby where my bridal party was waiting and I was killing them. I noticed even Sissy, standing there in a beautiful white summer dress that I was sure cost a grip had to give me her nod of approval. We never said it, but we both respected and appreciated each others sense of style.

We stepped out with me leading the pack and begin to pile into the 5 white stretch Navigators awaiting us and headed to the venue. My shit was being held at some over priced upscale lounge in SoBe. We began stepping out the trucks at had the whole block on stand still taking us in and wondering who we were..... if they only knew.

The Chandelier Lounge was 2 levels of pure luxury and beauty with a retractable rooftop. The set up was beautiful. Everything was white and black, the food looked and smelled amazing and the drinks started flowing as soon as we walked in. We had a nice dinner for the bridal party and THEN the Bachelorette party got underway. We had the whole venue to ourselves, and once the guest started to arrive I was glad we did cause it got packed pretty quick.

We danced, we drank, had a gift opening ceremony that was crazzzy and then FINALLY the entertainment arrived. 25 of the hottest male strippers the world had to offer. These bitches Ciaira and Shane flew niggas IN to send me off into marriage land right. Nothing but hard bodies, sexy faces and big dicks came stomping into that room. I was so glad I opted to wear pants because they wasted no time making me a part of their opening act. Where all 25 of them niggas as they were introduced, came out and "introduced" himself to me. After the formal introduction, there were 15 dudes who came out and worked the floor and then we had the final 10 headliners. It was definitely a night to remember. However I didn't cut up as bad as I wanted to because well as you know, my soon to be mother in law was right there. And although the way she was screaming after dick and grinding on niggas young enough to be her grandchildren.... I knew the bitch had a watchful eye on me. Waiting on me to fuck up so she could swoop in and speed dial her precious son. I hated this bitch at times, but I had to deal with her. In less that 24 hours I was marrying her son. She came with the package.

We partied until a little after 3 and then headed back t the hotel. I had less that 12 hours before the *moment of my life happened. I slept until about 8:30am and when I got up, shit was already in full swing. The suite was packed with my bridal party running around like chickens with their heads cut off. I had just enough time to grab a shower and swallow some tylenol and OJ for my hangover. We left at 9:45, headed to Key West for my wedding. I was filled with a mixture of excitement and too much liquor from the night before. I could only imagine how hard my husband to be had partied.*

Since we didn't have time to actually have breakfast, we stopped at McDonald's and grabbed some breakfast sandwiches and coffee etc and ate on the road to the wedding. When we got there, the staff was all set up and we had to jump straight into go mode. The very top level of the mansion was a buzz with women getting their hair, nails and makeup done. Squeezing about to get into those dresses. I was fine, at first, caught up in the laughter and excitement of the getting ready. Then, it was kinda like an alarm went off and told my jitters to wake up.

I was an hour away from marrying the love of my life. I felt like I was gonna throw the fuck up. I wasn't this nervous on our first date. But for whatever reason, knowing that in 60 minutes our forever would beginning.... man. Don't get me wrong, I was head over heels in love with Juan, 6 days out of the week.... cause keeping it real.

Although we could wipe our ass with thousand dollar bills, we were a real live couple. And yes we got on each others fucking nerves at times. So although the day changed, one day a week I was still in love... but my heels would be flat on the ground.

I walked around the room lost in my own thoughts and worry. My main fear was what if he got bored with me. What happens when the glitz and glamour was gone and I was just me. Would he still love me as he did today. What about the day I became old and gray. Then I wondered about what I was gonna feel when he got fat and bald..... who the fuck was I kidding. He was distinctly cut from Ian, and that was a sexy ass old man. And I was cut from Dana, and although my mother had spent time trading her box for cash, and crawling round the floor of our old apartment looking for what she "THOUGHT" she saw in the carpet.... and lets not forget standing in the living room fucking up the blinds, in the dark sucking on a straight shooter cause she soooo paranoid BUT she got to keep getting high.... even though she had been through all of that, Dana was a BAD. And having what seemed like endless cash on deck only made that bitch badder. And I was her first born.... me getting old and fucked up was not in the cards. If she could survive crack and still have even young niggas drooling, I could survive LIFE and keep that soon to be husband of mine walking around with his tongue dragging the floor.... at least I hoped I could.

I was pacing the floor when I heard a knock at the door. My heart felt like it literally STOPPED because I didn't know who was at the door. I was so scared somebody was coming to tell me Juan changed his mind or something. And when the door creaked open and I saw who it was, I was almost certain that was the message."

Sissy eases into the room and closes the door. Keeli is standing in front of the large open window looking out over the water. Keeli turns around and looks at Sissy, preparing for the worst. Sissy smiles at Keeli after seeing the terrified look on her face. "Don't tell me you about to jump."

Keeli wipes away the tears that are forming in her eyes. "Nah. I was just looking out at the water."

"It's beautiful. But honey, it's 2:10. You need to get inside that get up and lets go have a front seat view of the ocean."

"Ok." Keeli says with a cracking voice. She walks over to the table and grabs some tissue and starts to dab her eyes. Sissy looks at her and sighs then walks over and hugs her.

"Nervous?"

"As Hell." Keeli replies with a chuckle as her tears fall freely.

Sissy leads Keeli over to the oversized chaise and they sit down together. "Talk to me then."

"I was just thinking. What if he wakes up one day and decides he doesn't love me anymore. What if we get bored with each other, or what if.......

"Girl calm the hell down. You about to give yourself a heart attack with all this nonsense."

"It could happen. Hell you and Ian divorced and I've heard about how strong y'all love was."

"Me and Ian are not you and Juan first of all. And secondly......" Sissy holds Keeli's face in her hands lovingly so she can be sure she is taking in all she is about to say. "For as long as I can remember, I have watched Juan change women like he changes clothes.... FREQUENTLY. But believe it or not, I saw a huge change in him when you came bopping into the picture. I used to think he would never settle down. End up just like his silly ass daddy. But he surprised the shit out of me."

Keeli chuckles. "Me and you both."

"I know me and you haven't always seen eye to eye Keeli. And yes I gave you a hard time..."

"Tell me about it." Keeli laughs and Sissy hits her hand playfully.

"And for that I apologize to you. I just didn't want to see my son get hurt again. You will understand in a few years when CiCi starts bringing them through the doors.

"Oh lord. Don't remind me we coming up on dating season."

"See you scared already." Sissy teases.

"But seriously Sissy, I love Juan with all that I am and......"

"I know you do Keeli. I just had to make sure you were genuine and your intentions were good. But I am glad him and TiTi have you."

"Really" Keeli asks with a huge kool aide smile, glad to finally have Sissy's approval.

"Yes. And I'm glad to have you as my daughter in law." Sissy hugs Keeli tight sealing their new found bond. "Now get dress, I'm going to find a makeup girl to come fix your face AGAIN.... its time to get married honey."

"Ok." Keeli beams, unable to hide her smile.... not that she wants to.

"Of all the women in that Mansion that day, I never ever ever would've thought Sissy would have been the one to talk me down off the edge. Shit, I always thought she would be on the ground chanting JUMP with the rest of the motherfuckas who hated my guts. It took years, and 3 grandkids for this woman to finally bestow her approval upon my ass and call me what you want but I was happy and gonna work to keep shit solid between us. Yeah, I wanted my mother in law to love me... a quick way to keep the peace and keep my husband smiling and that's what was important.

I went about the task of getting ready to take center stage.... literally. Then my makeup artist showed up to put my face on fleek once again. Not that the expensive ass makeup we were rocking ran when I cried.... but knowing that I had been crying, that shit would've had me sub consciously freaking out about it. So she fixed me up and it was time. I stood there looking at myself in the floor to ceiling mirror and I was amazed. I was a beautiful bride. As I stood there admiring my wedding attire, I got the lets go knock on the door and with a huge smile, I opened the door and stepped out to go get married.

I made it down the 3 levels of the mansion they called a clubhouse and there was the wedding party.... all except the Preacher and the Groom. They all looked at me in astonishment, cause as I was told so many times that day, I was breathtaking. My girls went over me from head to toe making sure I had my something old..... The locket Juan brought me on the day we met. My something New...... A pair of Diamond Earrings I brought just for this day. Something borrowed. A bracelet from my best friend and sister from another mother Ciaira. And my something blue... My garter.

My escort down the aisle, the almost man who was giving me away stepped before me and he just smiled. CiCi kissed my forehead and told me I was the most beautiful girl in the world. From there, the coordinator started getting us in line for the wedding march. I looked at the wedding party and they all looked like perfection. Now I absolutely couldn't wait to lay my eyes on my husband to be.

Our wedding theme was the Garden of Eden.   There were exotic plants and flowers placed all along the private area of the beach that we were getting married on. It was a part of the estate that the mansion sat on. All the chairs for the guest were green and wrapped with exotic flowers. Like seriously, the flower tab on this wedding alone was bananas. There was a green grass runner like thing that laid the way from the bottom of the stairs, across the white sand beach down to the stage area. We had photographers set up to get shots of the wedding party as they came down the aisle as well as the guest. Me and Juan also had personal photographers that were to keep their cameras trained on us throughout this day. The wedding party were instructed to wear all white and they had to remove their shoes upon arrival. No stuffy suits, No hot ass church dresses. Keep it light and simple, and they did. I mean we were getting married on a private beach in Key West in June. They would've melted in that shit. But they all looked on in awe as the 2 trained white tigers made their way down the aisle. They would sit on the sand in front of the 2 stages during the wedding march, and once I joined my husband on *the center stage, they would be allowed to roam free. Yep, just wander around wherever they pleased... or so it looked. They were actually being guided by their trainers. Even though they were harmless at this point in their lives and were more like big ass house cats instead of ferocious jungle animals, they were beautiful mood setters. So were the exotic snakes that were exploring the trees. I wanted an elephant but the owners of the Estate said absolutely NOT. They were already taking a chance on us and our damn tigers. So the show went on without stampee. But the birds, snakes and tigers set the mood just right, along with the flowers and apple trees. We had a huge apple tree flown in that sat behind the center stage and shaded us. The tree was fake, but the apples were real.*

Juan stood under the tree with the Reverend on the center stage and he looked amazing in his white linen pants and no shirt. I couldn't wait to get to him. Since he knew he was gonna be shirtless during our wedding, he worked out like a prisoner for the last 6 months leading to this day.... him and all his groomsmen and MAN. This nigga body was cut up. Straight STREDDED. I knew every woman in the crowd was watching him like OH EM GEE. But all that was MINE. I smiled at the thought just as Glenn Lewis started to sing his rendition of the Luther Vandross wedding classic, "Here and Now" and watched as the wedding party made their way down the aisle.

My Maids of Honor were first down escorted by the Best Men. Simply put, Ciaira and Syrus escorted by Roc and Mickey. My girls were wearing long grass skirts and white lace tube tops. The guys like all the guys in the wedding, wore linen shorts and no shirt. Which is why Juan FORCED them niggas to workout with him.

Next were the parents. Dana and Alvin came first, followed by Ian and Sissy. Our mothers wore white toga style dresses and our dads wore white Toga robes. Although Ian was sexy, I just was not about to have him and my dad walking around my wedding with old man ab hair on blast. They had to cover that shit up.

They were followed by what looked like a sea of bridesmaids and groomsmen. 10 each. You already know what the guys wore, and the ladies wore these white tube dresses made completely out of exotic flowers. The shit was beautiful and well worth the money we kicked out for them allergy test before those dresses were made. I couldn't have none of them being taking out on stretchers because we didn't take the proper precautions.

Next came the ring bearers, Mecca and Ishmel. Both wearing white Toga robes like their grandpas because I didn't want their shit hanging out either. They were followed by my Jr Bride Infiniti. She wore a long white toga style dress made of tropical flowers and was escorted by Adovia flexing his ab muscles. They were followed by the lone flower girl, Asha, and she wore a dress made of tropical flowers also. Once Asha made it to the front, and found her place next to her daddy because she refused to stand where she was SUPPOSED TO.... Glenn Lewis took his bow as the guest clapped and then took his seat as the band begin to play and the legendary Miss Anita Baker took the stage and begin to sing "Giving You The Best That I Got." That was my cue. My handsome son dressed in nothing but linen shorts like the rest of the men took my hand and led me down the winding steps into view of everyone. They all stood to their feet and looked at me in awe as me and my son begin to make our way towards the love of my life. I never took my eyes off of Juan and his smile told me he couldn't wait to hear me say I Do. I took every step with pride wearing a short tube style white linen dress with a train that stretched back sooooo long.

I was so nervous at first, but as I took my rightful place by that man's side, all of my butterflies went away. I knew I was right where I belonged and so was he. The Reverend said his peace and then me and Juan recited our own vows we had written for each other. That was his idea and it was shocking. But his words were from the heart and left me shedding tears of happiness. I know my words pulled at his heart strings also but he would never cry about it. Instead he looked at me so intensely and let me know he heard me loud and clear and felt everything I was feeling. Finally the Rev announced us man and wife and he kissed me like he had waited all his life to do that. He scooped me up in his arms and took off down the aisle as our guest stood and cheered us on and took pictures and threw rice at us. We gathered with our entire wedding party inside the Mansion for photos before we all got changed for the reception. Once me and Juan got our kids together all changed and out the way, we found ourselves alone in the huge room I got dressed in consummating the marriage and it was fucking awesome. After a quick wash up in the bathroom, we got dressed and joined the rest of our wedding party downstairs to head off to the reception.

Like everyone else, me and Juan wore pure white. That was kinda the theme of our wedding weekend. The wedding party rode in a couple of stretch Navigators while me and Juan rode in a Cinderella style carriage being pulled by two huge white horses. Our guest had already been escorted to the reception via shuttles.

Our reception was held on a big ass yacht in the middle of the water and we all had a ball. Me and my husband showed everybody how you got fucking married. From the all-expenses paid invitations, to the star studded entertainment. Even on the yacht at the reception we had Backyard Band LIVE, And both Anita Baker and Glen Lewis performed again. And of course we had a DJ. At one point in the night I did feel a little sad for a second. I never thought I would be having a moment this big without BJ right in the middle. Then throw in that I was missing CoCo and Tiff and I can't even front, I missed Monae too. Kia..... nah. Ok Not as much as everyone else. But what was done was done. To drown out the sadness, I focused on having the time of my life and I did.

The next day, me and Juan were at the airport to personally say goodbye to all our guest. All 400 of them. We passed out Goody Bags and Thank you cards for them celebrating our day with us. I was exhausted by time we made it back to the hotel, but I couldn't sleep good yet because we had to be at the airport at 6am for the longest flight ever.

We spent the next 30 days in Dubai with some of our closest friends and relatives and NO KIDS. It was one of the best vacations me and my husband ever took together. I was sad when we had to leave, but I missed the shit out my babies at this point.

On the flight back home, I tried to wrap my mind around my first task the minute we got stateside. Telling Juan I HAD to come back to the streets. I had to do it quick too because we were scheduled to leave for our new permanent residence in Santa Monica on the 21st of August..... Not even 30 days. We already had a buyer for our home in Long Island and they were just waiting for us to come back to the U.S so we could sign the papers and get the fuck out. I wanted to talk to him while we were in South Africa BUT between funning with the family, seeing the land.... like we really went and visited the true blue slums and I realized that back in those days I was sleeping on a back porch and we was feasting on Noodles because that was all there was to feast on..... I was STILL BLESSED compared to what some of these people had to endure. Wasn't no crack epidemic over there to help their shit take flight. So between doing charity work, because KJCR Charities definitely wrote some 6 figure checks over there during that month. But between all of that, I didn't want to ruin the time we did have together talking business. Once we landed and cleared customs and claimed our luggage, I prayed for the perfect time to talk to my husband about the matter at hand.... and it fell right into my lap......

Or so I thought."

"Break Up To Make Up"

Keeli and Juan walk into their home followed by the driver and his assistant who make 3 trips bringing their luggage into the foyer of their home. Keeli busies herself in the sitting room going through the mail while Juan waits patiently for them to bring in the last bag. He tips them both 100 dollar bills and then locks the door after they leave out with gracious smiles on their faces. He walks into the sitting room and collapses on the sofa next to Keeli and puts his head in her lap.

"Damn if feel good to be home!" Juan exclaims with excitement as he kicks his shoes off and stretches his legs out on the sofa.
"Tell me about it. AND we don't have to look at no kids for the next 7 days."
"Ayyyyyyeeeeee."
"Ayyyyyyyeeeeee I know you better get your feet off this damn sofa Ayyyyyyeeee." Keeli jokes with Juan and hits him on his forehead with the stack of mail. "But seriously baby, you know what we should do?" Juan instantly flips over and begins trying to unbuckle Keeli's shorts and bite her legs. Keeli pushes him on the floor. "No fool. I was thinking, its been over a month since we really just got to be alone." She gets down on the floor and straddles him and kisses his lips softly. "Let me cook us a romantic dinner. I'm talking wine, candles, the whole nine. And we can just relax. Soak in the hot tub ALONE and just enjoy each others company."
Juan looks up at Keeli seriously. "That's what you really wanna do?"
"Yes Papi."
"Alright, do your thang. I'ma go upstairs and lay down for a minute."
"Ok. Do you want anything particular because I gotta go to the store anyway."
"Nah. I got everything I need right here with me now."
Juan kisses her softly on her lips. "I love you Keeli."

"I love you too Papi" Keeli leans down and returns Juan's kiss, with an even more passionate kiss of her own.

"I had all intentions of heading to the market, but hearing him say he had all he needed in me broke down my resolve. He picked me up and carried me upstairs to our bedroom and we fucked each other right on to sleep. When I woke up it was 5:30pm but his ass was still out. He was already jet lagged from that flight, then I put that snappa on his ass. Poor baby couldn't do nothing but sleep. I slipped out of the vice grip he had been holding me in and went and jumped in the shower. I slipped on some jean shorts, a tank top and some flip flops..... all Chanel and went downstairs to the kitchen. I checked our messages while I looked through my cookbooks for something different. I mean I was tryna butter him up for my big announcement so I needed everything to be on point.

After I decided on dinner I grabbed my Chanel Bag off the counter and went to the garage.
I decided since it was nice day to go on and whip my Birthday present from Juan that had only hit the streets twice. My white on white 2002 Mercedes Benz S500 AMG coupe. With all the customizations he had done to it, the price tag was well over 100 grand, but that was play money to us.

I drove downtown and went to grab the things I needed for dinner, then there was this lady who had a shop where she made her own scented candles, flavored lotions etc. I stopped by and loaded up on candles, massage oils etc because tonight I was pulling out all the stops. I planned for my last stop to be this little bakery that made thee best strawberry cheesecake from scratch in the whole wide world, but when I realized the time I knew by time I got in, cooking was out the question. So I went to my favorite seafood restaurant and grabbed us 2 lobster dinners to go and headed back home.

When I got in Juan was just getting out the shower, so I had time to get everything set up. I plated our dinner, lit candles around the hot tub and turned the jets on full blast. Then in the living room, I had the fireplace going just for ambiance, and a blanket laid out in front of it, and the massage oil and a bottle of Grey Goose chilling in an ice bucket waiting for us. When Juan came downstairs, I was laying on the blanket in nothing but my panties and bra and he couldn't help but smile at the way I had it set up.

We ate, hit the hot tub and relaxed and just shot the shit about nothing and had a few drinks. Finally we made our way to the blanket in front of the fireplace and I went for the kill with the massage. Juan had told me before I had magic fingers and whenever I broke them out..... I wanted something. I was trying to take a deep breath and just get down to business but the words just kept getting caught up in my throat. Finally I rolled him over and straddled him and began to massage his chest. I looked down at that man I realized how silly I was being. I had to just spit it out. Juan loved me and there was nothing in this world I couldn't talk to him about...... Nothing in the world he wouldn't stand by my side on.

Boy was I WRONG."

"Baby. I need to talk to you about something." Keeli says while continuing Juan's deep tissue massage."
"What's up Mami. I'm listening."

63

"Ok. So you know that I love you, and I ALWAYS take everything you say to....."

Juan gently grabs her hands and sits up. "You know I hate speeches. Get to what's on your mind."

"Ok." Keeli gets up off the floor and grabs her drink and downs it then sits the glass on the mantle above the fireplace. "I decided that I'm not gonna sell my company after all. It's been a whole bunch of crazy shit going on and I just can't bail on my peoples like that. So I decided I'm gonna give CoCo back her money and then I'll step back in charge." Keeli finally exhales. She walks back over to Juan and kneels down in front of where he is sitting on the blanket. "I know you said you want me to give it up but baby I can't. Not right now anyway. Not until I find somebody qualified enough to be my successor."

Juan grabs his drink and finishes off the glass then stands up. Keeli stands up and continues her speech while Juan sits his glass on the mantle next to hers. "So I was hoping that instead of moving out to Cali right now, we could go back to DC. Just til I straighten this shit out then we screaming West SIIIDE" She jokes as she crip walks to Juan. She grabs his hand and looks in his eyes. " I wanted to talk to you about this way before now, but I didn't want to spoil our honeymoon by discussing business. We were having such a good time and all. Baby I hope you understand why I had to do this." Keeli leans forward and kisses Juan softly on his lips. Juan takes a deep breath and then slaps the cowboy shit out of Keeli. Keeli falls back into the glass end table knocking off the crystal lamp. The lamp falls to the floor and breaks.

"All of a sudden you wanna move back to fucking DC huh!" Juan's voice booms and fills the room. "DC aint cross your fucking mind until you found out that bitch ass nigga was home!!"

"Baby what are you talking about?" Keeli asks from her new position on the floor cowering beside the sofa in shock. Juan closes the distance between him and Keeli before she can get her scream out good. He grabs at her and she slips out of his grasp like a greasy pig and haul asses through the foyer and up the stairs. She runs into the master suite and jumps across the bed and runs into the bathroom and slams the door because Juan is right on her heels. Juan begins to kick the bathroom door like a madman until finally the wood bends and the door breaks. He charges into the bathroom causing Keeli to get stuck between the wall and the door. He pulls her from behind the door by her hair and begins to beat her all over the large bathroom while accusing her of fucking Jackie.

"They say hindsight is 20/20, and I most certainly believed it because I didn't see this shit here coming at all. After only being married a month, here I was getting my ass beat by the man I loved. The one thing I said I would NEVER stand for was happening to me. The thing he promised he would never do.... he was doing.

After he finished his attack on me, he went and got dressed without saying a word and just rolled out. He left me laying there, damn near naked on the bathroom floor crying my eyes out. When I finally became unparalyzed by fear, I got up off the floor and made the mistake of looking in the mirror. I didn't recognize the person who sat before me. This wasn't the beautiful, confident Keeli that usually greeted me with a smile. The chick I saw was WEAK with a capital W. A straight fucking mess. Standing there, eyes all swollen... right one damn near closed. Fucking bruises and shit all over me. Lips swollen and busted. I hated her. I hated this bitch here so much. The one thing I could not stand and would not tolerate in my life was a weak ass individual.....

So why was I becoming her?

While I stood there, talking myself up about how as soon as my eye heal I was done with his ass and was breaking the fuck out, taking the kids, filing for divorce etc. While I popped all that shit trying to convince the chick staring back at me in the mirror..... Inside. In my heart, I only wanted my husband to come home. Tell me he was sorry, promise to never do it again. Hold me close and kiss away the pain. I know back in 95, I swore on everything that if he ever breathed at me hard again I was gonna put a fucking bullet in his head without question.

That shit was easier said than done. He was my husband. We shared 3 fucking kids and a last name at this point. So while I talked all that tough girl shit trying to hype myself up, inside I was dying.

I spent the next 4 days in the house alone. Calling this motherfucka AT LEAST 100 times a day. Leaving message, after message, after message BEGGING him to come home. I couldn't eat. I was sleeping in spells. I was a mess. Ciaira and Roc hadn't been over because I guess they were catching up on alone time. I didn't call because I didn't want anybody knowing what was going on in our house. Not even our best friends.

I woke up on the 4th day to find out that my hideous eye had gone down. Since I hadn't showered brushed my teeth or combed my hair in four fucking days, I decided it was time to get it together. I filled the tub with bubbles and water as hot as I could stand it and put the jets on blast and relaxed. I had to pull it together. Once I finished my bath, I called the girl in Queen's who did my hair and she told me to come on through. I was hell bent on being extra cute this day because I needed the confidence booster. I had just been beaten and abandoned by my husband so my confidence was in the shitter. After going back and forth on what to wear, I settled on a three tone cream, brown and blue Gucci summer dress that looked more like a long blouse with a belt. The shit was hot and the immediate confidence booster I needed. I stepped into my cream Gucci gladiators with a 3 inch heel, threw on my aviators, grabbed the keys to my Range Rover and hit the streets. I was gonna get my hair done, head to Manhattan and do some shopping and just take it one day at a time.

Cara was my hair dresser and my cousins girlfriend so we chopped it up a bit, I told her all about Africa. Showed her and the girls some the amazing flicks from the honeymoon. Cara had been at my wedding so she had already showed them hella pictures of how BOSSES wed. Finally we got down to the business of my hair. She asked me what she was doing with that stuff and I told her just cut the shit off. She thought I was playing but I was dead ass. I was in a drastic mood, so I went for a drastic change and had her cut my healthy shoulder length hair down to a boy cut. I had never in my 27 years of living had a haircut so it was emotional as hell for me and I cried. Not just for the hair that was falling but for me and all I was feeling inside. After it was cut, I got my shit died. I went from Jet Black to strawberry red. It was different, but it was HOT.

When I left the shop, every nigga on the Ave was tryna holler. It may sound shallow as hell but it was truly the confidence booster I needed. Since it was a nice day out and I was feeling myself I drove into Manhattan for some retail therapy. I was working the shit out JUANS card too. Once I was done, I hopped in my truck and headed home.
When I got in, I just knew by me not calling Juan at all that day.... he was gonna have called home since he hadn't bothered to call my cell. So I was beyond pissed to see I was wrong again. So I called him one last time and went thee fuck off. No baby come home, blah blah blah. I was like nigga FUCK YOU. I called him everything but a child of God. Then I told him he didn't have to worry

about coming back because I was done with his ass and I would be gladly collecting my shit and leaving in the morning. From there I got undressed, crawled into bed and cried myself to sleep. I woke up about 2 hours later because I had to Pee and I was starving from the J I faced on the drive home from the city. I was in the bathroom when I heard this idiot come busting in the house, screaming my name like a mad man. I was in fuck him mode so I didn't budge. I handled my business.... washed my hands and walked out the bathroom and ran smack into his stupid ass."

Juan stops in his tracks when he sees the drastic change Keeli has made to her appearance. Keeli snickers at him. "Oh I see you finally found your way back huh." Keeli attempts to walk around him and he pulls her back. "What the fuck did you do to yourself?"
"I got a haircut. Oh what, you don't like it?"
"Fuck no."
"Well good thing it doesn't matter since I"M LEAVING YOUR FUCKING ASS." Keeli attempts to walk away again and he grabs her by her waist and pulls her back to him. "So you just gonna bail on a nigga Ke?"
"Nigga you fucking HIT ME!" Then you rolled out for FOUR FUCKING DAYS! No calls, No text, No NOTHING! So hell yes. I'm leaving your ass!"
"I fucked up Ke."
"NO SHIT!"

"Look, can we just sit down and talk about this." Juan ask humbly.

"Ohhhhhhhhhhh" Keeli laughs in his face. "NOW your motherfucking ass wants to talk. When I mention leaving your ass, you can find your way home AND your words. But when I wanted to talk, all you could find is your motherfucking FIST!" Keeli punches him as hard as she can in his chest causing him to stumble back.

"I deserve that."

"No, I'ma show you what the fuck you deserve!" Keeli walks into the huge dressing room/closet and starts packing her clothes erratically. Juan walks into the closet with tears in his eyes.

"Keeli, you are my wife. You are NOT leaving me. It's as simple as that."

"Motherfucka WATCH ME!"

"I fucked up alright. I fucking love you and I thought I might lose you if you go back to DC. I love you too fucking much to let you go. Especially to some bum ass nigga who had his fucking chance and left yall.

Keeli throws the arm full of clothes she is carrying to the floor. "That's what this is about? Fucking Jackie! You think I want Jackie Juan? You are fucking RIDICULOUS!" Keeli walks over to him with tears rolling from her eyes and jabs her finger in his face. "Since the day I met your arrogant ass, All I have fucking wanted was YOU! How dare you think somebody could take your fucking place. My heart is with you as it always has been with you."

"Ke listen."

"No fuck that YOU LISTEN JUAN! I'm your wife, true enough but I'm also a business woman just like you are a business man so I would THINK you would have a little more understanding of where I'm coming from." Keeli walks over and sits down on the chaise. "The shit CoCo and Tiff pulled is foul. And at the end of the day my name sits on all this shit. And aside from that, Ty, Donna and all them are my peoples Juan. That's my family. And while I

would never choose them over us, I would never abandon them either. I'm all they got for real."
Juan walks over and sits beside Keeli and holds her hand.
"You right baby. I was wrong for the way I acted. Especially for accusing you. I hope you can forgive me. And to show you how real I am about righting this wrong with you, we can go ahead and go back to DC TEMPORARILY."
"Are you serious Juan?" Keeli tries to hide her smile from spreading across her face.
"Temporarily Ke. And you can go back to SUPERVISE. You can't be out here getting caught up in the middle of all this shit. The risk are way too high.
"I can deal with that." Keeli beams with delight.
"So you forgive me?" Juan pulls her close to him.
"You wish." Keeli playfully pushes him away. Juan grabs her playfully and pulls her over the chaise and down to the floor on top of him and they begin to kiss.

"Whoever said makeup sex was the best sex ever aint never lied. Juan was determined to let me know just how sorry he was for the shit he did. I'm talking toe sucking, ass licking, back biting, cum til you cry sex.

When we were done, Juan carried me to the tub and we took a hot bubble bath together. As I laid on chest letting the water ease away my stress, I felt my eyes begin to fill with tears of sadness. I loved Juan, but after what he had done to me 4 days ago... I just didn't know anymore. I mean that was the 3rd time I felt pain from the hands of the man who said he loved me. Why wasn't I

71

strong enough to leave or demand he get some help? Maybe I was over thinking shit. Maybe it wasn't as bad as I was making it out to be. Maybe that was the last time he would hurt me.   Now before you go getting all smart assed and shit bringing up everything I said about Dana when she used to go through this shit, let's get something clear. First this is different. Juan is my husband..... Dana aint never been the wife of NA NIGGA who hit her. So that alone made it different.

Or at least that's what I tried to tell myself.

Once our bath was done we climbed into our bed and Juan just held me close. I could feel the guilt eating him alive. I turned over and looked at him and saw my husband battling with something inside himself. He needed me.... just like I needed him. I kissed his lips and told him I loved him as I closed my eyes and said a silent prayer for us, then I slowly drifted off to sleep. And after 4 days of wandering this house and laying in this bed hurt and alone, if felt good to listen to the beat of my husband's heart against my ear.

The next day Roc and Ciaira came over for dinner. We fired up the grill, ate good, drank good and played spades. Me and Juan smiled and laughed and loved as always.....

My best friend had no clue to the nightmare I had just experienced 5 days ago. Over spades we talked to them about DC and they agreed to come down with us that weekend. We had to pick up our kids and find a house. Ciaira was happy that I wasn't going all the way to Cali just yet, and I know the kids would be happy about going back to DC. That's where our family was. This way they could spend more time with their cousin and shit while I tended to my business. So I knew everything was gonna work out fine.

On Friday morning, the 4 of us left Long Island, DC bound. Me and Ciaira in my Range Rover and Juan and Roc in his. We all stayed with Sissy that weekend and I went and kicked it with my mom and the family on Saturday. Dana, Her boyfriend Kevin, Lamai, Her boyfriend Ant, Adovia, My Aunt Fran and my cousin Crisshawn were all living in my house in Columbia. Dana had kept Ishmel and Mecca for me when they got back from the wedding and my babies were sooooo happy to see their mommy walk through that door.

On Sunday Morning we went and looked at a list of properties and me and Juan fell in love with an Estate in Potomac Maryland. It was about 30 minutes from Sissy house and an hour flat to DC. It wasn't as big as my place in Long Island..... but that bitch wasn't small either. It had 7 bedrooms, 5 full bathrooms. A huge pool. 4 car garage and a huge finished basement with a theater room and all. There was a play area for the kids but no basketball or tennis court like our home in Long Island, but there was definitely enough land to add that shit if we wanted it. We agreed to take it.

At dinner that night, me and Juan of course had to keep pushing until our besties said they would make the trek to DC with us for the time being. We wasn't ready to break away from our go to couple just yet. And besides, I needed Ciaira with me to help clean up the mess them bitches created, and oh what a mess it was. We extended our trip until Wednesday so that Ciaira and Roc could lock down a house also.

The boys all got back from Basketball Camp on Monday night and I was so happy to see my baby that was soooo not a baby anymore. CiCi was 13 and stood at 5'10.... towering over me. His little mustache and shit was growing in. Voice was getting all deep. I looked at my son and marveled at how handsome he was. He was like the perfect combination of me and Jackie..... I began instantly anticipating the bullshit.

Ciaira and Roc chose their house on Tuesday. A 5 bedroom, 4 bathroom spot in

Germantown Maryland. They wanted to be close to Roc's mom for the kids sake which made sense. Same reason we moved close to Sissy......... On call babysitter. We didn't tell any of the kids about the move until we got back to New York and they were hyped. Well CiCi and Infiniti were. Mecca, Ishmel and Asha really didn't give a shit either way. All they wanted to know was if their toys were going to the new house.

We spent the next two weeks focused on packing up the house. I was so excited about getting back to DC. I had been hella busy in New York with my business ventures but being busy did not stop me from missing my family and my team. The movers were scheduled to arrive the next morning, which was Friday to get our shit and take it to DC. We were gonna stay at a hotel in the city, then on Saturday, the painters and cleaners would do their thing and on Sunday morning we would be meeting the new owners at the house to hand over the keys to the fortress. From there we were headed HOME

That evening, me and Juan held our last dinner at our house for everybody that was there. We had brought up some relatives to help us get packed and then drive 10 cars back to DC. About 10:30 that night, me and Juan were chilling on the sofa together in the family room watching TV and trying not to fall asleep because we were exhausted from the past 2 weeks. The twins and Asha were asleep, Ciaira and Roc were gone home Lamai, Infinitie, and Juan's niece Samantha were at the basketball court watching Ant, CiCi, Adovia and Robby play ball. And Mickey, Earlie and Teddy had gone into the city to hit up club Twinn. So the house was quiet and empty. Me and Juan were just enjoying a quiet we hadn't had in about 2 weeks...... then we got a surprise neither of us asked for or expected.

So here is some food for thought. If your doorbell ever rings late at night, and you know you not expecting any company..... don't answer it. Just grab your glock and start shooting cause whoever is on the other side is a problem, and always remember, DEAD MOTHERFUCKAS CAN'T CAUSE NO PROBLEMS."

"Maranda"

Juan is laying on the sofa and Keeli is laying between his legs with her head on his chest trying so hard not to let the TV end up watching her. Juan leans down and kisses the top of her head and asks "You ready to go to bed?"
"I guess so. We got another busy ass day tomorrow."
"Yeah I know. But you wanted this."
"Hush Juan. Go ahead and get up."
"Nah, you get up and then pull me up."
"Same time."
"Alright. On my count... 1.....2.....3....." Keeli gets up off the sofa and Juan stretches his legs out further. Keeli hits him in his arm. "Come on Papi, you playing too much."
"Shut your whining ass up. I'm coming now." Juan gets up off the sofa and turns the light off. He walks out of the Family room and into the foyer with Keeli right behind them. They get halfway up the stairs with the doorbell rings.
"Oh my God. Who the fuck is it?" Keeli groans.
"I don't know, but you closer to the bottom of the stairs so you get it." Juan takes off up the stairs.
"Bastard!" Keeli yells at him as she turns and starts walking back down the stairs. She walks down to the French Doors and opens one of them. A beautiful Latino woman is standing there wearing a short white sundress, white stilletos and her long dark hair is flowing down her back. She smiles a warm and beautiful smile at Keeli.
"Hello. I'm looking for Juan."
Keeli looks at her incredulously. "And you are?"
"I'm Maranda."
"Maranda? Is that supposed to mean something to me?"
"Well no, not to you I don't guess. Can you just tell him Randi is here. He will know who it is." Maranda smirks.
"Yeah alright." Keeli slams the door in Maranda's face and walks to the foot of the stairs.
" Juan! Get the fuck down here NOW!" Keeli stands at the foot of the stairs waiting for him to appear, shooting daggers with her eyes and tapping her foot to try and

calm herself. Juan comes out the master suite in his pajama pants and Asha is right behind him.

"What the fuck you yelling for yo?

"Why am I yelling? Really? Just tell me who the fuck is Randi and why the fuck is she at my door asking for you smirking and shit Juan?"

"Randi?" Juan's eyes light up like a Christmas tree. "Stop playing Keeli."

"Do it look like I'm playing! Asha GO TO BED!"

"Don't yell at her!" Juan picks Asha up and walks down the stairs and heads towards the front door.

"I asked you a fucking question Juan! Who the fuck is Randi and why is she at my door?!"

"That's TiTi's fucking mother Keeli!"

"Now I aint never been the jealous type. It just wasn't in me. But KNOWING that some bitch who knew his fuck faces well before me, AND had carried his child well before me was standing on the other side of our door had me feeling some type of way FOR REAL.

I had never met the bitch. Didn't know shit about her. I never even knew the bitch name until now. He never mumbled a word about this ho and I never asked.

Why?

Because I didn't care. She was no threat to me. Outta Sight, Outta Mind.

But now the bitch was IN SIGHT and IN MIND. And now I wanted to know all about her.... starting with why the fuck she was at my house at almost 11 o' clock at night looking for MY HUSBAND. What the fuck was her motivation? I didn't know but I was damn sure gonna find out even if a motherfucka or two had to get hemmed up in the process. I gave no fucks at this point."

Juan puts Asha down and opens the door. A smile about as long as the Brooklyn Bridge spreads across his face when he sees her.
"Hoooooola Papi!" Maranda beams with delight and out stretched arms.. "You gonna just stand there looking silly or give me a hug?"
Juan steps into her embrace and hugs her as they both smile."Look at you Ma. You looking good girl."
"So do you Papi. You been working out?" Maranda squeezes his biceps.
"Every now and again." Juan begins to flex his chest muscles causing Maranda to giggle and blush. They finally step back from each others embrace. "Come on in Randi."
"I thought you would never ask." Maranda grabs her large rolling suitcase and steps into the house and Juan closes and locks the door. Keeli and Asha are standing next to each other and Keeli's eyes are as big as golf balls as she stares at the two of them in disbelief.
"Oh wow." Maranda says breaking the silence. "You have a beautiful home Papi."

"Thank you. This is all courtesy of my leading lady."
Juan pulls Keeli next to him. "You met my wife Keeli right?
"You are married?"
"Yep. Were still newlyweds." Juan beams with pride.
"Oh well congratulations to you both. Maranda quickly turns her attention back to Juan. "I just can't get over how good you look. You got the pecks going on and stuff."
"Cut it out Randi. I always look good and you know it. Why don't we go in the family room and sit down."
"Yes, we have so much to catch up on."
Juan picks up Asha and holds Keeli's hand as they walk back into the family room and Maranda follows them, leaving her luggage in the foyer.

"For the next 45 minutes straight, I sat there listening to the two of them talking. I had nothing to say because anything that came out of my mouth would be ugly as fuck like the bitch shoes and ultimately lead to violence. So I just listened. I listened to everything the bitch said closely, and even closer to everything the bitch DIDN'T say. She went on and on about her career as a fashion model in Paris. And how she was bored with the whole thing now. According to her, that is why she decided to come back to the states.

Yeah fucking right. I wasn't buying that shit.

No Sell.

While they talked for that 45 minutes, and she went out of her way to keep reminding me that she was a fashion model. One thing stood out to me and it stood strong.

NOT ONCE.....

NOT A SINGLE FUCKING TIME

Not even briefly did she mention her daughter. Not even to ask where the fuck the child was at, at damn near midnight. And this silly motherfucka Juan, just sitting there grinning and laughing with the bitch. Yeah I was on FIRE. My insides were smoking at that point. But even though I wanted to jump across the room and choke that bitch to DEATH, I held it inside. I sat and held Asha until she fell asleep. Then I got fucking tired of the trip down memory lane. It was late and beyond time to wrap this shit up. Bitch needed to get her little rolling luggage and get the fuck on where she was headed."

"Baby, it's getting late. You wanna go get the kids from the basketball court?" Keeli interrupts Maranda and Juan's conversation.
"Yeah you right. Time was just getting away from me."

Just them Samantha, Eric, CiCi, Infiniti, Robby, Adovia, Lamai and Ant come running into the backdoor pushing

each other and running through the house. Infiniti is running towards the family room "Ma! It's a racoon on the tennis court!" Infiniti crosses the threshold into the family room and stops in her tracks when she sees Maranda. The rest of the gang come in behind her. "That joint was big as shit too." Eric continues.
"Boy watch your damn mouth!" Keeli snaps at him.
Maranda smiles at Infiniti who is still standing stuck as if she has seen a ghost. "Hi Baby." Maranda walks over to Infiniti and hugs her. "Oh my God. You have gotten so big. And Beautiful."
"What are you doing here?" Infiniti asks not really knowing what to feel about her mother's presence.
"I came to see my baby girl."
Keeli looks at the rest of the crew who are standing there waiting for the fireworks. "Don't y'all have something else to do?"
"Hold on, let me introduce everybody to you." Juan gets up and walks over to the group. "This is Earlie son Eric. Roc son Robby. Juanita's daughter Sam....."
"You so silly Papi. You acting like I don't remember them. I used to change Robby and Sam's diapers. Sam you were my daughter before I even had a daughter."
Maranda chuckles in a attempt to make her comment seem lighthearted, when it was really about establishing who was here first.
"My fault." Juan chuckles. "It's just been so long since you seen them."
Maranda smiles and looks at Juan. "No matter how long you are away. You never forget your family."

Almost everybody in the room takes a step back anticipating Keeli attacking Maranda. Even Juan is surprised when she doesn't move. He continues with his introductions. "This is my son CiCi. My sister in law Mai, her dude Ant and my my brother in law Dovia.
"Hello." Maranda says through a forced smile.

"Um, Ke, we about to go to bed." Lamai says while giving her sister the "just say the word" look.

"Ok. Can you lay Asha down in my bed please?" Keeli hands a sleeping Asha off to Ant. Him and Lami leave the room followed by Robby, CiCI, Samantha, Adovia and Eric. Keeli sits on the Chaise and Juan takes a seat on the sofa. Maranda sits next to him and Infiniti squeezes in between them. Maranda grabs Infiniti's hand and smiles.

"I can't get over how much you have grown baby."

"You still haven't told me what you are doing here." Infiniti cuts in.

"I came to see you baby. I was missing you so much Infiniti it was making me sick. So I gave up modeling to come back here and be with you.

"Y'all got a lot ot catch up on Randi. I'ma go get us something to drink. Have you ate already? We got burgers, chicken, potato salad.

"Wow. That sounds delicious. I could stand a bite."

"Alright. Baby you wanna come help me out in the kitchen?"

"Excuse me?" Keeli looks at Juan unable to hide her distaste any longer.

"Come help me in the kitchen." Juan goes over and pulls her up from the chaise and down the hall into the kitchen with him. Keeli closes the sliding kitchen doors to give them privacy and leans against them with her arms folded across her chest. Juan starts taking the food out of the huge sub zero refrigerator and looks over at Keeli who doesn't look happy at all. "What's wrong Mami?"

"Don't call me that shit now more. And why the fuck is she here, in my home after midnight?"

"Oh so it's YOUR house now?

"Don't even try that shit. Answer my question. Why is this bitch here?"

"She came to see her fucking daughter Keeli."

"I can't tell. She spent the last 45 fucking minutes grinning in YOUR fucking face." Keeli snaps.

"So what you timing her?" Juan asks Keeli as he is unable to hide the scowl on his face.

Keeli picks up on his change of demeanor quickly and softens her tone. "Look, it's late and we have a bunch of stuff to do tomorrow and I'm past ready to go to bed."

"Then go to bed! I know my way upstairs!"

"Oh and leave you and that bitch down here all alone? I don't fucking think so."

Juan turns from the plate he is making Maranda and looks at Keeli in disgust. "You don't trust me huh. I fucking married you and you don't trust me."

"It's not you I don't trust Juan."

"You know, I can't stand an insecure woman Keeli."

"Insecure!"

"That's how the fuck you acting! I married YOU, NOT HER and you standing her fucking bitching about nothing. You aint see me tripping when your bitch ass baby father was tryna come to our fucking wedding!"

"I didn't ask him to come Juan. I didn't even fucking know he was out and you know that!"

"And I aint ask her to come here either! Juan throws the serving spoon into the sink causing Keeli to jump. He grips the counter with force to try and calm himself as he counts backwards from 20. Once he feels calmer, he walks over to Keel and tilts her chin so he can look in her eyes. He sees she is on the brink of tears. "Look Ke. Me and Randi have known each other since we were kids. We are like brother and sister."

"Brother and sister who just happen to have a baby together huh." Keeli pulls away as tears start rolling down her face.

"So what you want me to do Ke? Go put her out? Tell her she can't see her daughter? What? Tell me what to do in Keeli's world?

"I didn't say that! I said it's fucking late and I want her out of my fucking house Juan!" Keeli snaps.

"Man look." Juan goes back over to the food and continues to make Maranda's plate. "You tripping. Go

upstairs and lay down. You tired and talking out the side of your neck and I'm trying to contain myself right now but you making that hard as fuck to do!"
"Oh so you gonna hit me now?"
"Man shut the fuck up Keeli!"
"No! I'm speaking the truth and you know it! That bitch aint here to see no fucking TiTi and as long as she in my goddamn house I'M UP!" Keeli pushes the sliding doors apart and storms out the kitchen and back down the hall towards the family room. She stops short of the entrance and counts backwards from 100 to calm herself down When she finally stops shaking from a cross between anger because of the situation and fear that Juan was gonna hit her, she walks back into the family room with a confident smile and takes a seat on the chaise. Maranda and Infiniti are looking at Maranda's photo album.

"Dang Ma, you have met everybody. It must be fun being a model."
"It was baby. But I couldn't stand to be away from you any longer. I missed you like crazy mama." Maranda kisses Infiniti on her forehead. Infiniti smiles up at her. "I missed you too Ma."
Keeli rolls her eyes at the mother/ daughter display of affection that she doesn't believe is real. "So Maranda.....
How long are you gonna be in New York?"
"Permanently. Europe was fun and all. They partying, the celebs, the shopping, the sights...."
"I've been. Quite a few times." Keeli smirks at her.
"Well all of that was fun. But there is no greater feeling than watching your children grow up. I am sure you know that."
"Of course I do. I've been with my children since day one. Nothing has EVER come before them."
Maranda is caught off guard by the low blow and takes a minute to gather her thoughts. "Did you guys just move in? I noticed all the boxes and stuff."
"No. Actually we are moving out." Keeli smiles at her.

"Yeah Ma, We are moving back to DC."

"Really? When are you guys leaving?" Maranda asks with a disappointed look plastered on her face.

"Sunday. Day after tomorrow." Keeli smiles at her knowing this news is unraveling whatever true plans brought Maranda to her door.

"Oooh Ma! Why don't you come with us?" Infiniti suggest with excitement. It will be fun. Grandma Sissy and everybody is there."

"Yeah Sissy would love to see me. When I talked to her she actually wanted me to come there first. Now I see why."

"Oh you talked to her?" Keeli inquires.

"Oh yes dear. She is the one who told me where to find Juan at." Maranda smirks as in saying CHECK MATE BITCH to Keeli.

"Come on Ma please. I think it will be a good idea." Infiniti pleads.

Juan walks back into the family room carrying a plate of food and a glass of lemonade for Maranda. He gives it to her and sits on the chaise with Keeli. "What would be a good idea Ti? What got you all excited now?"

"If Ma was to come back to DC too. That way we could spend more time together."

"Ti, I know you wanna be close to Maranda and all." Keeli starts "But she can't just leave her place and I'm guessing job here in New York. But you will still get to spend time with her.... I promise." Keeli smirks at Maranda

"Actually I'm ok to leave." Maranda begins. "I haven't found a place yet. I just flew in from Paris today. I came straight here from the airport because I couldn't wait to see my baby." Maranda smirks harder.

"So where will you stay tonight Ma?" Infiniti asks with concern.

"I was hoping your dad could recommend a good extended stay hotel. I was gonna stay there until I find a place and get settled. But I honestly wouldn't mind going

back to DC." Maranda looks at Keeli. "That is, if you all don't mind me hitching a ride down with y'all."
"You don't mind, do you daddy?" Infiniti asks with excitement.

All 3 women in the room have their eyes focused on Juan waiting for a response. Infiniti sees his hesitation and pulls out her secret weapon against her daddy. She gives him her sad, I'm about to cry face because you saying NO to me will only shatter my heart into a million pieces look. Juan takes a deep breath and looks down at the floor. "Nah, I don't mind." Infiniti screams with excitement as she jumps up and runs over and dives on Juan and starts kissing him all over her face. "Thank you sooooo soooo much Daddy! I'm soooo Happy! We gonna have so much fun Ma. Come on let me show you my room." Infiniti jumps up and runs back over to Maranda and grabs her by the arm and pulls her up. Maranda giggles with delight as she follows her daughter upstairs to her bedroom.... where she will be staying the night.

Juan takes a deep breath and prepares for the unavoidable fight that is coming. "Baby....." He begins to plead his case.
"Go to hell." Keeli gets up and walks upstairs and Juan follows her quietly. She walks into their master suite and slams the door in his face. He comes in the room and closes the door behind him.

"Baby listen....."
"Don't you fucking baby me."
"Ke just listen to me please."
"You don't have shit to say to me and I fucking mean that nigga." Keeli goes into the dressing room and starts undressing. Juan comes in behind her and grabs her by her arm forcefully.
"You are my fucking wife Ke! I married you! Don't you fucking remember that?" Juan tilts her chin and looks

into her eyes trying desperately to reach the understanding layer of her soul. " I chose you Ke. Out of all the women in the world I chose you. Because I love you. And I want you Mami. I'm not checking for Randi. I'm not checking for nobody but this little baldheaded lady standing in front of me."

"Then why....... Keeli starts to question him."

"I'm doing this for TiTi. She wants to spend time with her mother. She wants to get to know her mother, and I don't think we should deny her that."

"I'm nothing saying deny her anything Juan. But what's gonna happen when we get to DC? She gonna stay with us there too? Try and take my husband while under my damn roof? She already stealing away my little girl."

Juan hugs Keeli and kisses the top of her head. "Baby aint nobody stealing nothing from you. Me and Ti gonna always be here."

"You say that now."

"Keeli do you love me?"

"You know I do."

"Do you trust me?"

"It's not you I don't trust Juan."

"I didn't ask you that. I asked you if you trust me."

"Yes. I trust you with my life."

"Then stop stressing over shit that aint gonna happen in this lifetime or the next. It's Mami and Papi forever."

"How I know you mean that?" Keeli asks trying not to smile at him.

"I said it didn't I?". Juan kisses Keeli on her forehead. "And besides, I'll just let her know what happened to the last broad who tried to steal something from you. If you going like that about money, I don't think she even tryna find out how you would go about your family." Juan jokes.

"Damn right." Keeli laughs.

Juan squeezes her butt. "Now come on and let Papi ease that stress for you."

"Boy." Keeli pushes him off of her playfully. "Do you not see your daughter right in the middle of our bed?"

"Who said anything about a bed?" Juan walks over to the dressing room door and closes it and turns off the light.

"I don't even have to say what happened next..... you already know the deal. So moving on.

The next day I was a tad bit more relaxed because Juan was right. He chose me. He made me his wife. And truthfully speaking he could have any woman in the world he wanted. And he wanted me. I refused to let this bitch think she was winning. So while I tucked my tude in my back pocket, I kept my eyes and ears peeled. She had a motive for being here and my women's intuition told me it aint have jack shit to do with Ti.

I loved Infiniti as if I had gave birth to her, and raised her as such. So as much as it stung, I respected her wishes to get to know her egg donor better despite my despise for the bitch. Ciaira and Lamai was tripping off the whole situation and ready to eat this ho alive. None of us could understand how any woman could give up her child. Fuck I was dirt broke, on welfare but my son still had me. So nah, that shit wasn't registering with us too well.

From what Juan told me, the bitch had been our of TiTi's life since 1993. So why now.... 8 fucking years later do you miss your daughter sooo much you can't stand it? This bitch was definitely playing games, and I was determined to find out what games exactly she was playing and beat that bitch to death with the board. I wanted to beat that fucking phony ass so called Mother in law of mine ass too. How dare that bitch hand off my address to this bitch like it was ok. Sissy knew she was outta pocket for not following the chain of command on that shit. She was supposed to take down that bitch info and then call ME and put me on and let me run it to Juan and we take it from there...... not send this bitch on what could've been a suicide mission for her. I aint have no words for that Jamaican slut after that. And here my dumb ass was thinking the moment we shared before my wedding was genuine and special. HA.

Fool me once, your ass wont fool me no more cause next time you try, yo ass will get SHOT.

So to keep from having to kill my own husband and everybody else I had grown to love of the years as family, I decided that the wall between me and Sissy was going back up ASAP. Fuck her and Maranda.

The movers came and got our shit and we went to the hotel. Saturday the cleaners and painters were doing their thing. Sunday we passed off the keys to our home and by 2pm we were on the road in a 10 car convoy heading to DC.

Once we got there, I kept a low profile the rest of August. I was busy getting the house together, enrolling the kids in school and shit of that nature. Just adjusting. Maranda stanking ass went to stay with Sissy but I wasn't surprised. I knew her true colors so I didn't trip. I mean the bitch damn sure wasn't staying with us. I loved TiTi ass to death but that was where I drew the line in the sand. She was pissed, because before she could get that shit out her mouth good, I shut it the fuck down. She threw a bonified tantrum like that was gonna change something. I wanted to knock her fucking noodles loose, standing in my damn kitchen, screaming and carrying on because I wouldn't let some bitch who her father USED to fuck lay up in my house. I was her fucking mother, as I had been raising her ass since the day her father walked his ass through the door. I had never hit her but I was damn sure about to. But I guess Juan was fed up too because he took a belt to her ass and then grounded her for two weeks straight. She was hot as a pistol, but her ass would have to deal.

Other than those little family hang-ups, I was happy. I was back in my native land and I had to get shit right. After a long ass 5 year hiatus, The Queen had come home to claim her castle.

It was time to show these motherfuckas how you run an empire.....

AGAIN!"

"Taking Care Of Business"

September 2003

Keeli is standing at the center island in the kitchen finishing up making lunches for the kids. Juan comes into the kitchen and hugs her from behind and kisses her on her neck.

"What's up Mami?"
"Good Morning Papi." Keeli blushes.
"You coming down to the club today right? The promo people for that ladies night bash coming today, so you need to be there since this shit is your idea."
"What time?"
"We set for 1'o clock."
"I'll try to be there by then. I got some stuff I need to...."
Juan turns Keeli around and tilts her chin so she can look directly into his eyes. "Don't try. Be there."
"Ok, I'll be there."
"That's what I like to hear." Juan turns Keeli back towards the island and smacks her on the butt. He pours himself a glass of orange juice and downs it. "I'll take CiCi and Ti to school, you got the rest of the crew right."
"Yeah."
"Cool. So I'll see you at 1."
"Ok."

Him and Keeli share a kiss and "I love you's" then he heads out the kitchen to get started on his day. After Keeli finishes packing the kids lunches, she goes downstairs into the basement into the area her and Juan have dubbed as "the vault" It's a huge closet that has a bank vault type security door and access code that only the couple share. Inside the vault, there are Multiple industrial safes stacked floor to ceiling around the room along with a shelf that holds multiple money counters, a table and 4 chairs. Keeli walks over to the table and grabs the two oversized duffle bags and struggles to take them one by one upstairs and to the garage entrance off the kitchen.

"Ishmel, Asha, Mecca Lets Go!" Keeli shouts for the children who are in the family room watching cartoons. She struggles to get the first bag holding 25 million dollars CASH inside of it outside and places it in the back of her Range Rover. She walks back into the kitchen at the same time as her 3 children enter dressed in their Navy Blue and White Private School Uniforms.
"Get y'all lunch boxes and meet me in the truck." Keeli struggles to pull the second duffle bag out the house. The kids grab their lunch boxes and backpacks and they walk into the garage just in time to see her struggling to hoist the bag in the back of the truck.

"Mommy what's in there?" Asha asks innocently.
"It looks heavy." Mecca chimes in.

Keeli stares at the two large bags of dirty money in her trunk that she is about to deliver to CoCo as a refund and shakes her head. "The story of her demise baby..... The story of her demise."
"What's a demise mommy?" Asha inquires.
Keeli snaps out of her trailed off thoughts of CoCo and Tiffany and what will more than likely become of them. "We can look it up together after school. Now come on and let's go. Chop Chop." Keeli rushes to help the kids get settled in their seats and then she hops in on the driver's side, opens the garage door with the remote, starts the truck and drives away.

"After I dropped the trio off at school, I started making my way to Upper Marlboro with a heavy heart. I loved my cousin and my sister, but they had let the devil and his

sidekick in and now I couldn't fuck with them. I had to worry about me and my family, and that day as I stood face to face with Simm after all these years, I could see the hate he felt in his heart for me from a mile away. Jackie was different. I don't know what the look was he held in his eyes, but being the way shit had played out I wasn't tryna find out. So while I loved Tiff and CoCo, I was forced to love them from a distance.

I think I must have been on auto pilot all the way because I got to CoCo's house so fast and I truly don't even remember the drive. I pulled up in her driveway and chuckled at how things had changed. I knew this big stupid ass house was Simm's call. All the time me and CoCo got money in these streets together, my cousin stayed in the same house she grinded on a pole and hustled hard in the trenches to get. I mean fuck she handed me 50 mil so she HAD money, but she always loved her humble home. But this big stupid motherfucka here. It was all him.

They now resided in what one would call a circle house. It was an actual circle at the back of a cul de sac. It was beautiful, but it wasn't her. From my understanding, she copped this the minute I put that crown in front of her. I'm talking about 8 bedrooms,

AN ELEVATOR, Olympic sized pool, 6 car garage. Gourmet kitchen and all. There were about 10 houses that sat behind the gated community that overlooked a huge golf course. And of the 10, this monster was the biggest. What tickled me the most was that I had to stop at the guard's gate and they had to call up and get her Ok for me to come to her house. Once I was given the Ok, I drove along taking in the scenery. These motherfuckas was living better than ME out here.

I got out and walked up to the huge double doors and rang the doorbell and waited patiently. I chuckled to myself as the 5 minutes ticked away and I thought back to what Ciaira said as we waited outside that big ass Presidential Suite..... It gets kinda hard to hear in these big motherfuckas. Just as I finished my reminisce, CoCo opened the door and the sight before me was kinda scary. She had dropped enough weight to cause notice. If you hadn't seen her in awhile, you would give her the "Is she smoking..... or got that shit" look. She aint have on shit but a silk bath robe that was still tryna work past its retirement. It had a big ass stain on the left shoulder that I was afraid of. Her hair was fucked up. Like the weave in it quit long ago but she was too fucked up to notice. My heart broke looking at the disaster standing in front of me."

"Hey boo!" CoCo damn near yells with excitement. "What you doing here?"
"You aint gonna invite me in?"
"Oh yeah. I'm tripping. Come on in."

Keeli walks into the house and it looks as bad as CoCo... just shit everywhere. Keeli follows CoCo down the hall into the kitchen, being cautious NOT to touch anything along the way. They get to the kitchen and the counter is covered with dirty dishes, the sink is filled to capacity, the floor is dirty and sticky . The garbage is overrunning and the entire house smells of stale air and cigarette smoke. Keeli sits down on one of the bar stools that doesn't have anything on it.

"Why don't you open a window or something?" Keeli asks while making the stank face.
"I am. I was just about to start cleaning up when you showed up out the blue." CoCo rolls her eyes and starts taking the dishes out of the sink. "So what you and the family down here for a visit?"
"Nah, not exactly. But sit down we need to talk."
"Go ahead, I'm listening."
"Nah, this is serious. Your fake clean up spree can wait..... motherfucka been dirty all this time."
"Damn, you just gonna come in my damn house and just GO huh."
"Man shut the fuck up and sit down! Like I said this is serious and I'm pressed for time."
CoCo starts to pat the pocket of her robe. "Please tell me you got a cigarette on you Ke."
"You know damn well I don't smoke. The fuck is wrong with you yo?"
"My bad Ke, damn." CoCo uses her had to smooth out her robe. "So look, when the next shipment coming in? My peoples ready to get back to work baby."

"CoCo, do you remember anything that happened in Miami? Keeli stares at CoCo in disbelief."
"Girrrrrlllll!" CoCo chuckles. I was so fucked up in Miami. Don't be mad boo, but I swear I don't even remember being at your wedding." CoCo chuckles harder.
"That's because you wasn't!" Keeli snaps. "What the fuck is up with y'all yo! Seriously this shit is fucking sad!"
"What you talking about Keeli?"

"You and my fucking sister! Y'all all fucked up, strung out on that shit!"

"Wait a minute! I aint strung out on a motherfucking thing! I don't know who the fuck you getting your info from cuz, but you got me fucked all the way up with this shit!" CoCo starts patting her robe again. "I need a fucking cigarette."

"CoCo, nobody told me shit. I can look at you and tell your ass is geeking right now." Keeli says sadly.

"Nah baby, not me. I'm good and aint geeking for shit."

"Yeah ok. Look I aint come here to debate if you do or don't get high. I came over to give you your money."

"What money?" CoCo asks with wide eyes.

"Your 50. I got it in the truck." Keeli stands up. "So what I need from you is the keys to the warehouse."

"Oh. Um......."

"Um What CoCo?"

"We sold the warehouse."

"What! Why the fuck....... Look, never mind, I aint even gonna get into this today. How much CoCo?"

"How much what?" CoCo ask dumbfounded.

"How much you fucking sell it for!"

"Oh. 300."

"Ok, so where is my money?"

"Oh, I invested it. Me, Tiff, Simm and Jackie decided......"

"You gave them niggas 300 thousand dollars of my money? Bitch I KNOW your ass getting high now! You fucking gotta be!"

"I keep on telling you I don't fucking get high! I didn't give them anything! It's a fucking business investment!"

"Investment in what?! Their motherfuckin pockets! How the fuck could you be so stupid!"

Just then the door chime goes off alerting them someone has come in the house. Simm starts walking down the hall. "Babe, where you at?"
"I'm in the kitchen" CoCo yells back to him.
"Who got the big boy range sitting out in the driveway?"
Simm walks into the kitchen and stops in his tracks when he sees Keeli standing there. "Well well well, if it aint miss married lady. Miss Big Shit. Miss Money Bags."
"Fuck you Simmeon."
"Baby did you bring that?" CoCo asks while rubbing her temples.
"Yeah I got you ma." Simm looks back to Keeli and smiles. "So what you doing here?"
"I aint come to see yo ass that's for sure."
"She came to take the business back from me." CoCo cuts in.
Simm chuckles and looks at Keeli. "Ke, don't you think you taking this envy shit too far baby?"
Keeli burst into laughter. "Envy of what? Negro please."

"Look, I know finding out about Tiff and Jack had to be a hard pill to swallow. Then add Me and Co on top of that and I know....."

"Nigga." Keeli laughs and then takes a moment to regain her composure. "Let us get some shit straight right now. Tiff and CoCo are my blood. My sister and FIRST cousin, so I'ma ALWAYS have love for them......" Keeli looks at CoCo. "Even if they is strung out."

"I keep telling you....." CoCo tries to interrupt.

"Shut the fuck up, I'm still talking!" Keeli turns to face Simm. "But y'all. I don't give a fuck about no Jackie..... And I don't give at minimum 10 fucks about yo bum ass."

"Bum!" Bitch I made you! When you was dirt broke and fucked up out here in these streets, I took care of your ass! If it wasn't for me, your ho ass would still be sitting around waiting on your fucking welfare check and food stamp cards!" Simm snaps. "Bitch you wouldn't have SHIT if it wasn't for me!"

"I'm glad you think that, but sweetheart, I was born for this shit. So I was gonna make it to where I'm at now with our without your little funky ass 100 grand. That wasn't about nothing. Nigga I'll give you a fucking refund RIGHT NOW....then what!

"Hold up." CoCo walks and stands in the middle of Keeli and Simm. She looks at Simm confused. "You gave her a hundred thousand dollars Simm?"

"Shut the fuck up CoCo." Simm moves CoCo out the way and she jumps right back in his face. "Fuck no! You gave this bitch a hundred fucking thousand dollars but I gotta fucking beg you for a hundred dollars and it's MY fucking money!"

"I said shut the fuck up!" Simm slaps the shit out of CoCo, knocking her to the dirty kitchen floor. "You see what the fuck you made me do!"

"I'm sorry baby." CoCo cries from her place on the dirty floor.

"Fuck you bitch." Simm walks out the kitchen and heads to the door. CoCo scrambles to get up off the floor and takes off running behind him.

"I stood there just taking all this shit in. My girl was completely gone. Strung out AND stupid as fuck chasing after this bum ass nigga. Now before you get all on your soapbox talking about I got some nerve, remember this. The shit that happened between me and Juan was completely different. He's my husband. No I'm not saying that makes him hitting me right, it's wrong for any man to lay his hands on a woman but........

Wait a minute....

What the fuck am I explaining myself for? I'm the Queen Of DC, I don't have to explain shit to you madam/sir reader.

So moving on.

I walked outside and watched the antics of "Coked Up Cathy". I stood in awe as she made a complete spectacle of her herself. She all out in the driveway in nothing but that stanking ass robe, crying, screaming, banging on this nigga truck. Straight begging this motherfucka not to go. I couldn't believe the shit I was seeing......

and I know the other occupants of this exclusive ass community were peeking out windows and doors, clutching their pearls in awe at the shit unfolding in the driveway of that big stupid ass house at the back of the cul de sac.

I swear this bitch used to be some of everything, and now she was all of nothing.

Word to Jesse Jackson we needed a true blue "Up With Hope, Down With Dope" Rally Right here, right now. But I knew as well as everybody else that it was too late for her. Shit like this was why I was teaching my kids to JUST SAY NO.

Drugs were a motherfucka FOR REAL.

I watched literally with tears in my eyes, as my cousin lay halfway on the ground, holding on to the door of Simm's Ford Excursion crying for him not to leave her and screaming that she was sorry. He pushed the door with so much force and hate that it hit her in the face, knocking her completely to the ground with her little dirty robe showing off what used to be the body of a goddess.... now it was the body of an addict. It was no way I could stop the tears from falling. Somewhere inside I felt it was my fault my cousin had this monkey on her *back these days. But wasn't nothing I could do.*

Simm stamped what I already knew when he yelled at her "Stay the fuck away from me you dopefiend bitch" and then proceeded to toss a huge ziplock storage bag of snort on the ground at her. Then he mugged me in a way that told me, I needed to kill this nigga before he killed me and then he was gone.

I loved CoCo and wanted to help her, but at what cost. Being as though she had just performed in the hills of Crackerville and this nigga had just tossed enough work on the ground to make me miss Asha's high school graduation I had to do what was best for me so I handled my business because it was time to get the fuck."

Keeli opens the back of her truck and pulls out the two duffle bags and drags them over to where CoCo sat on the ground crying. "You really need to get yourself some help Co. For real. Get help." Keeli walks back to the truck and closes her trunk then gets in and backs out of the driveway and leaves.

"I cried for about a mile into my journey the fuck away from that foolishness that just to

place. I really felt bad for CoCo. She was my blood, my first cousin. But you CANNOT help a motherfucka who don't want to help themselves. I was feeling like Bobby Womack when he sang that song Harry Hippie. So Much so I cranked it up from my Ipod and let it bump through the speakers cause I needed that right now.

I like to help a man when he's down. But I can't help you Harry if you wanna sleep in the ground. Sorry Harry... I think I'm gonna put you down. Sha la la la, sha la la lala. Sha lala la la la lala.

I may have just spoke a foreign language to you but I loved that song. I still remember my daddy used to play it when I was a little girl and it always stood out in my mind. I guess cause one day, I would know Harry Hippie.

I looked at the time and I had finished my first order of business and it was only 10:30. I didn't have to meet Papi until 1 so I had more than enough time to finish handling my business.

I knew it wasn't a wise choice, but I had to do what I had to do. If I was gonna put my peoples back on the streets. I had to make sure they were gonna be safe. So after almost 10 years, I was FINALLY gonna meet the man, everybody feared......"

"Daye"

Keeli pulls up in front of the community room of the apartment complex in Northeast where Daye runs his shop from. She hits the combination and the stash box raises from the center console. She grabs her gold desert eagle, checks the clip and then sticks it down inside her Gucci purse. She says a quick and silent prayer, then gets out the truck and walks straight towards the community room.

She walks inside and there are 4 guys playing football on the PS2 that is connected to a huge TV. 2 guys are playing table tennis, and a set of four, 2 guys and 2 girls are sitting at a table playing spades. One of the guys at the spades table stands up.

"Yo ma, the rec aint open yet."
"That's nice. I'm looking for Daye."
"You looking for Daye?" The second guy at the table stands up. "Yo who the fuck is you?"
"You aint Daye, So I don't see how the fuck it concerns you." Keeli snaps back.
"Watch your mouth shorty."
"Look, I came to see Daye, not his fucking yes niggas. So is he here or what?"

Just then Daye walks out the back office followed by his right and left hands, Smurf and Damion. He smiles when he sees Keeli standing there. "Well well, I aint expect to find this rare gem our here making all this noise."
"Yo Daye you know this bitch?" The first guy from the spades table asks.
"Chill the fuck out." Daye commands him then focuses his attention back to Keeli. He walks over to her and towers over her with his 6'3 would've gone to the NBA if he hadn't been grabbed by the allure of the streets frame and looks down on her. " So you looking for me huh? That's funny. Cause I was just about to start looking for you."

Keeli stares up into his dark eyes with the heart of a lioness. "Is that so? Well I'm here, so do you have somewhere we can speak in private.... without all your house niggas about and shit." Keeli stares at the two guys from the spades table. Day chuckles, amazed at the heart she carries and her disrespectful mouth. "Yeah ma, step into my office." Daye leads Keeli back down the hall to his office. They walk inside and he closes the door. Daye takes a seat behind his metal desk and motions for Keeli to sit across from him. "You got a lot of nerve stepping up in here. And a lot of heart talking to my peoples all greasy like that. What you crazy ma? It's cold blooded killers in that room." Daye chuckles.

"I can handle myself just fine. Trust me." Keeli taps her bag with a smile. "And nah, I'm far from crazy. But I came to speak to you...Them niggas don't even make my radar, so they need to learn their place when dealing with a boss."

"I feel you. But I'm here now, so talk."

"So it's like this, me and you done worked the same city, same hood for a hundred years with no issues at all. There was a mutual respect between us."

"You right." Daye interrupts, " I respected the fact that you respected my turf and stayed away from my peoples. Shit, I sent that nigga J-Man on the mission back in the day just to see if you was gonna fuck with him or respect a nigga position. You respected it..... Granted your girl didn't. But for your respect, I let you eat without gunplay. I mean, wasn't no secret y'all was fucking with a better supply and could've shut the shit down and forced me to kill everybody or go into early retirement. But you played fair so I let you do you. No tax, no nothing."

"And I appreciate that."

"Like I said, there was a mutual respect between us..... Was being the operative word in that statement."

"I'm hip. That's why I'm here now speaking to you."

"So speak. You aint said shit yet. Just stated what I already know."

"I'm not sure what went down with your peoples, and I'm truly sorry for your loss..."

"Keeli, it aint even about them hitting shorty. I don't give a fuck about that. You wanna know what really pissed me off about the whole thing?" Daye gets up and stands behind his chair. "I'm like Willie Motherfuckin Dee out this bitch. I make big money, I drive big cars, everybody know me, it's like I'm a movie star.

Keeli chuckles at his reference to one of her favorite Geto Boys songs. "Yeah. I know the feeling."

"So why do these two no name bitches think they can fuck with me?"

"Daye, that's something I really can't answer. I guess when you weak minded, motherfuckas can easily convince you to sign your own death certificate. But I'm here to let you know personally they aint running shit no more. I'm back on the throne.

"So what that mean?"

"Look....." Keeli stands up. "Your beef is with them. Not me and not my team. So I'm tryna make sure we got an understanding before my peoples get back on the block. Cause my guns bust just like yours."

"Alright. You got that." Daye says nonchalantly.

"Just like that huh?" Keeli eyes him suspiciously. "Just like that you gonna call off your hounds."

"Aint nobody to call off. I aint never really have them on the team. I just put them in a fucked up situation..... As long as them bitches was running the show, they couldn't get no money in my city point blank. But you...." Daye walks around the desk and stands in front of Keeli, so close that if he was naked, the hard on she has given him would've poked her in the stomach. "I like you. A lot." Daye winks at Keeli. "So we cool. Y'all can eat hand over fist just like the good ole days."

"And you aint even gonna tax me?"

"For what? We both sitting on bread like wonder. Me charging you a few slices aint gonna hurt you so why bother." Daye puts his arm around Keeli's waist and pulls her too him. "I tell you what you can do tho. Let me take you to dinner on my yacht. I just copped a mean ass joint. It's out Annapolis. Private Chef and all. Some good food, a few drinks and lets see what the night brings about."

Keeli blushes. "I'm flattered Daye, but you know as well as every other dude in this city, I'm married now." Keeli holds her left hand out so Daye can check out her wedding set.

"Dammmmn. That's what's up. But see that's why I like you. You stay playing fair."

"Aint no other way for me." Keeli winks at him. "But look, I have some other places to be so I gotta jet. But thanks for meeting with me Daye. I appreciate it."

"Anytime baby. Come on let me walk you out."

"I'm good, you don't have to."

"I wouldn't be a gentlemen if I didn't." Daye gently takes Keeli's hand and walks her out his office and outside to her truck. They exchange a hug and Keeli climbs into her Range Rover and leaves.

"This nigga had to think I was stupid. Your baby's mother done been kidnapped and murdered and niggas done came at you with a ransom..... And you just gonna step to the side and let me and my peoples back in the game?

Yeah right.

This motherfucka was just as grimy as I was so I had to watch him like a hawk. Especially now since he knew he didn't have a chance in hell of fucking me. He was fine tho with his bald headed ass. Now had this been back in the day, we could've linked up, fucked and got this money. But I'z married now. Although I was still gonna play him close.

Like they say, Keep your friends close and your enemies closer..... and I was gonna keep Daye as close as possible without getting raped in the process.

Since I was already in the neighborhood, I went to holla at Donna. I let her know we was meeting the next day. Then I made my way through the city and got with all the niggas on my team that mattered and gave them word on the meet the next day. And finally like the awesome wife I was, I was walking into the club at 12:59 for my meeting with Papi and the promo team."

"More Drama"

"Me and Juan left the club about 5:30 and headed home. I was tired because it had been an eventful day. Since we were in the city so long, CiCi and Infiniti took the school bus home and I had Dana pick up the goof troop for me. Now I had to get in the kitchen and make them pots and pans jiggle. Although I was tired as hell, I didn't mind. I was really into my role as wife and mother.

I made sure we had a sit down dinner together as a family ATLEAST 4 times per week. I had to make sure that even though we were all busy with our own lives we kept that Q.T flowing. Juan would always joke that we were like a new day version of the Cosby's. Our clan of kids were fairly good. I mean yeah they had their moments.... you know the moments where you look at them and think Damn, I should've swallowed your ass. But all kids have those so it was cool. Aside from awesome kids, we had cheddar and we valued our family above all. Only difference was, Juan ass wasn't no doctor and I wasn't no lawyer. We were them peoples. We controlled the game at this point. Cliff and Claire wasn't even hardly about this life.

We got home and my only intentions were to chill, cook and spend time with my family but that motherfucka name DRAMA was pulling up in my driveway right behind me

and the nigga had bags cause he planned to stick around for quite a while."

Keeli and Juan get out of their separate vehicles in the driveway and walk into their home. "What happened? All the kids moved out?" Juan jokes.
"Nigga you wish. I'ma go get changed and start dinner." Keeli takes off up the stairs towards their bedroom. After she changes into a pair of sweats and a tank top, she comes back downstairs and peeks in on Juan who is stretched out on the sectional in the family room watching ESPN. She goes into the kitchen and puts on her apron and starts to take the stuff out the refrigerator that she needs for dinner. Dana and kids come in the house through the sliding door that leads to the backyard. Keeli looks at the kids who are sweaty and look as though they have had the time of their lives. "Hey dirty butts. Where y'all been?" She inquires as she kisses each of them on their sweaty foreheads.
"Outback riding their bikes. Grandma getting too old for this shit here." Dana laughs.
"Ma your ass been old."
"Shiiiit. You wish. As long as my niggas aint complaining little girl..."
"Oh lord." Keeli laughs. "Little dirty kids, y'all stink. Go upstairs and take that stuff off."
"Is daddy home?" Mecca inquires.
"Yes. He watching TV in the family room." The three kids take off down the hall pushing each other the entire way while arguing about who is gonna get to Juan first.
"Thanks for picking them up for me ma."
"No problem. You need some help? You know Juan and the kids like my spaghetti better than yours." Dana jokes.
"Girl Bye." Keeli laughs. "My man aint checking for nobody spaghetti but mine. And the kids don't count."

"Yeah Yeah Yeah. Whatever. Well I'ma head on home, you know I hate driving out here at night."
"Cause you old and blind."
"Your baldheaded ass daddy." Dana and Keeli both laugh as Dana walks out the kitchen. "Call me when you get home ma." Keeli yells down the hall behind her.
"I'll think about it." Dana yells back jokingly from beyond the kitchen.

Thirty minutes later Keeli is making the salad for dinner while Infiniti is sitting at the center island telling her about her day at school. Ciaira walks into the kitchen. "Oooh, something smell good in here."
"Hey boo. What's up."
Ciaira sits down beside Infiniti and pushes her "Girl everything. What's up fathead."
"Hey auntie." Infiniti kisses Ciaira on the cheek.
"What you making? Spaghetti?"
"Yep yep. What you doing over here this late?"
"It aint late. How was your day?"
"It was interesting, but we will talk later." Keeli nods her head subtly towards Infiniti letting Ciaira know she is the reason she can't tell her about her day. "How was yours?"
"Stressful as fuck."
"You need a one on one?"
"Like nobodies business. Aye, I got a half of a J left in my purse. Lets go on the deck."

Keeli takes her apron off and throws it on Infiniti's head. "Finish cutting the vegetables for the salad for me." Her and Ciaira walk outside on the huge deck and sit next to each other on the picnic table. Ciaira sparks her blunt and takes a long pull. She lets her head fall back as she exhales the weed smoke at a snails pace trying to catch her maximum high. She hits it once more then passes it to Keeli.

"Alright so first Brooke showed up at our house at the crack of dawn on some bullshit. Talking about she want Robby to come and stay with her."

"Are you serious? So what y'all gonna do?" Keeli hits the blunt again and passes it back.

"I don't know. But that aint the worst part of shit. I get over to the shop and my shit done been broken into."

"What the fuck? Are you serious?"

"Yes. Motherfuckas done spray painted the walks. Cup up like 250,000 dollars worth of my winter line. So I spent the day fucking with the police and insurance company. And let me tell you about these bitches. According to them, my shit wasn't covered. The property and all my hard word just down the fucking drain."

"How is it not covered Ciaira? I was with you when you signed the paperwork and...."

"My policy wasn't to go into effect until the store officially opened for business."

"And what Roc say?" Keeli asks as she hits the blunt again.

"He can't deal with this right now. He got bigger issues at the moment."

"Damn baby."

"Then you know my mother and them got into town today."

"Oh yeah. They staying with y'all?"

"Nah. They wanted to be in the city so they at my aunt house. But once I finished with the stress of the shop, I went to go see them and my mother gave me this."

Ciaira pulls out a an envelope addressed to her from a Morgantown FCI.

"BJ?" Keeli inquires?

"Yes. He wants us to come and see him."

Keeli takes the envelope from her and looks at it. "So when you wanna go?"

"When you gonna have time? He said his visits are Tuesday, Wednesday and Friday"

"I'm meeting with the team tomorrow, so what about Wednesday? We can head out there after the kids go to school."
"Alright. But lets keep this between us. I don't need this getting back to Roc and then I'll have a whole new set of issues and shit to deal with."
"I feel you."
"And can you keep this letter for me?"
"Of course." Keeli takes the letter from Ciaira and puts it in her back pocket. "So what are you doing tomorrow?"
Ciaira puts the roach of the blunt out. "Going to the shop. Start to clean up this mess."
"Well I'll be done with the crew by like 1, so I'll come by and help you out."
"Thanks boo. I'ma go ahead home and take a shower and lay it down. This day has been a fucking doozie."
"Alright. Call me if you need me."
"I will."

The girls share a hug and then go back in the house. Ciaira walks down the hall to leave and Keeli washes her hands and gets back to cooking. At about 8:30pm, Keeli, Juan and their 5 kids sit down at the table in the dining room to have dinner. After the twins and Asha bless the food they all start making their plates and eating.

"So how was school today?" Keeli inquires as she starts putting salad in Asha's salad bowl.
"I'm glad you said that. I need one of y'all to sign this permission slip for me. It gotta be in by tomorrow." CiCi cuts in.
"Damn, school just started and y'all going on trips already?" Juan asks.
"Nah. I wanna try out for JV Basketball.
"Why JV? You ready for varsity. I taught you everything you know and I'm a monster on the court." Juan does a fade away shot from his seat with a paper towel and it lands in Keeli's Salad causing the kids to laugh.

"I don't qualify for varsity until I get in 8th grade then they go by skill alone."

"Alright. I'll sign it for you after dinner." Juan and CiCi give each other dap.

"Um excuse me." Keeli chimes in. "Don't I get a say so in all this?"

"Come on ma, please don't start tripping." CiCi grumbles.

"You better watch your damn mouth boy."

"Chill out Mami. I got this."

"Mommy..." Ishmel starts. "Where do you work at?"
Juan starts laughing. "Why lil man?"

"Because my teacher wants us to find out what kind of work our parents do and then we have to talk about it for career day.

"Oh ok." Keeli breathes a sigh of relief. "Me and Daddy are entrepreneurs.

"Anche who?" Mecca chimes in.

"Entrepreneurs man." Juan laughs at his son version of the word.

"It means they own their own businesses Ish." Infiniti clarifies it for her siblings.

"Well can I just say that cause I can't say that other word?"

"Yes you can baby." Keeli assures him. "But I still want you to practice saying it and eventually you will be able to say it. ok."

"Ok."

Juan cellphone starts to ring. He pulls it out his pocket and answers it. Keeli gives him a dirty look while taking in his one sided conversation. "Hello...... Nah, not really. What's up?....... When?...... Ok cool...... Give me like 30 minutes. Alright bet." Juan hangs up the phone and notices Keeli and Infiniti both are giving him dirty looks. "What's up. Why y'all goosing like that?"

"I thought y'all said no cell phones at dinner daddy."

"We did." Keeli snaps at Juan.

"Mannnn. Both of y'all shut up. I run this."

"Excuse me?"

Juan downs his glass of lemonade then gets up and walks over and kisses Keeli on her cheek. "I'll be back."

"I like your nerve Juan. You didn't even finish eating."

"Wrap it up for me Mami. I wont be long."

Juan walks out the dinning room. He grabs his keys out of the key bowl on the table in the foyer and leaves the house.

"I was feeling some kind of way about the shit he had just did. Your phone rings and not only do you answer it in the middle of dinner BUT you just get up and bounce? I was livid, but I wasn't gonna make a scene. I had a rule about showing my ass in front of the kids and it was simple.... I didn't.

We finished up dinner then CiCi and Infiniti cleaned the kitchen while I gave my babies a bath and got them ready for bed. After I got them all tucked in, I laid it down myself. I was tired but I didn't fall asleep until well after 1am.

And Juan still wasn't home.

I got up at 6am like I usually did, and guess what.......

JUAN STILL WASNT HOME.

So saying that I was pissed was an understatement. If a married man stayed out all night, you better believe it was between another bitch legs. I was ready to explode as I walked down the stairs to go start breakfast. This motherfucka was truly tripping if he thought this shit was ok. As soon as my foot hit the bottom step, guess who came trying to creep through the front door. His fake ass creep mode only served to piss me off more."

Keeli stops on the last step as Juan comes in and locks the door and starts talking off his shoes.

"I hope." Keeli begins. "No fuck that, I KNOW you not just coming home Juan."
"Come here...."
"No fuck that! I wanna know where the fuck my husband has been until 6 in the motherfucking morning!"
"Man, pipe down before you wake up the kids." Juan walks into the family room and lays down on the sectional.
"Pipe down my ass. You come strolling up in here THE NEXT DAY...."
"Keeli calm down. I went over Earlie house and then we all were helping Randi move into her apartment."
Keeli looks at Juan as if he just sprouted 8 extra heads.
"So you telling me you was with that bitch all night!"
"No, not how you thinking Ke. It wasn't just me." Juan tries his best to explain. "Earlie, Quincy. LaLa and Jeff was with me so it aint what you thinking baby."
"Whatever." Keeli looks at him in disgust and walks out of the family room and heads down the hall into the

kitchen to get breakfast ready for her children. At 8am, she walks back into the family room and wakes Juan up, her attitude still ever present. "Get up, I need you to take CiCi and Ti to school."
"What time is it babe?"
"2 hours later than the time you fucking came home."
"Come on Ke, cut that shit out."
"Whatever."
"Ti aint going to school today. I forgot to tell you earlier."
"And why the hell she not? She aint sick or nothing."
"I know boo. Randi asked me to bring her over to see her new place."
"And she couldn't do that shit after school? Or better yet on the fucking weekend!"
"Come on Keeli, it's way too early in the morning for this shit."
"Hey that's YALL child so do whatever. Fuck this shit."
Keeli storms out the room and goes to the foot of the stairs. "CiCi! Asha! Mecca! Ishmel! Let's go!"
Infiniti comes down the stairs before the other children ready to go to school "You forgot somebody." She kisses Keeli on the cheek.
Keeli returns the loving good morning gesture to her step daughter. "No I didn't baby, you not going to school today.
"Why not?" Infiniti ask giving the screw face.
"You gotta ask your father about that baby girl."
Infiniti goes into the family room to get answers from Juan just as the other children start to come down the stairs. "Y'all get your lunches off the counter and meet me in my truck."
"You taking me too ma?" CiCi inquires.
"Yes I am if that's ok with you. Now get your stuff and meet me in the truck please."

The kids all make their way down the hall into the kitchen. Keeli walks into the family room where Juan and Infiniti are. "Do you think you can find the time to pick them up from school this afternoon? I'm going to help Ciaira out at the shop."

"Yeah, I think I can manage that." Juan chuckles, refusing to acknowledge Keeli's attitude.

"Go to hell." Keeli walks out the family room and goes back down the hall into the kitchen. After she gets her purse she walks outside and climbs into her Range Rover where her 4 children are waiting. She drops the younger children off at school first and then heads in the direction of CiCi's school. CiCi turns the music down to get Keeli's full attention. "I'm glad you dropped them off first ma."

"Yeah. And why is that?"

"Because I need to talk to you about something."

"What's up baby? Everything ok?"

"Alright ma listen." CiCi hesitates trying to gather his words. "But you gotta promise you wont get mad."

"Spill it Jayceon!" Keeli demands.

"Alright. Ma I didn't go to school yesterday."

"What you mean you didn't go to school yesterday? Juan took y'all to school."

"He took us, but I didn't go in. I waited out front until the homeroom bell rung then I left." CiCi confesses nervously.

"What the hell is wrong with you Jayceon!" Keeli takes a deep breath and tries to calm herself before speaking to her son again. "I'm not paying 2500 dollars a month in tuition for you to be playing hookie CiCi. Running the streets and shit."

"I wasn't running the streets ma."

"So what the hell was you doing that was so important you had to ditch to get it done? Do tell CiCi, do tell."

"I was hanging out with my dad." Keeli looks at him in disbelief, trying to process the news he had just given her. "You know Jackie. My biological father. Remember him?" CiCi says sarcastically.

"Don't be a fucking smart ass Jayceon!" Keeli snaps as she drives onto the school grounds. Instead of driving into the drop off area, Keeli pulls into a parking space and turns the truck off. She takes a deep breath and counts backwards from 20 before she speaks. "CiCi, what were you doing with him? How the hell did you even get in contact with him?"

"Aunt Tiff. When we was down North Carolina at basketball camp, they came down one Saturday for a visit. He called me on my cell yesterday morning and said he wanted to see me. So I went and saw him. I mean he is my father ma."

"You think I don't know that CiCi."

"He said he wanted to spend time with me while we were all down Miami but knew you was gonna trip so he stayed away until he knew you were out of the country." CiCi laughs.

"So he didn't think asking you to skip school to see his dumb ass was gonna make me fucking trip!"

"Ma, I'm just trying to be honest with you and tell you what's going on cause I don't like lying to you or keeping things from you. But I like him. And I want to get to know him better out in the open. Not on no sneak tip."

"Excuse me!"

"Ma, I'm just saying. He's my father and I think I have the right to get to know him and spend time with him if I want to."

Keeli turns to look at CiCi and points her finger in his face. "First of all LITTLE BOY, you are 14 years old. You have no fucking rights. Let's get that understanding FIRST!"

"But y'all let Ti see Randi!" CiCi snaps back, regretting he ever tried to be open and honest with his mother.

"If it was up to me, Ti wouldn't see her stankin ass either. Her father allows her to see that bitch. But understand this I am YOUR MOTHER, and what I say in regards to your ass goes. You feel me?"

"Yeah Ma." CiCi turns to look out the window so Keeli can't see the tears welling up in his eyes.

"I don't want you going anywhere near him anymore PERIOD! And to make sure of that, give me the phone CiCi?"

"Come on ma, you trippin!"

"Give me the GODDAMN PHONE JAYCEON!" Keeli snaps at him, yelling loud enough to cause a few passing students to look in their direction. CiCi takes his cell phone from his backpack and tosses it on the dashboard in frustration. He goes in his pocket and pulls out a piece of paper and slams it on the dashboard beside the phone. "He wants you to meet him here at 10 this morning. He said he really needs to talk to you about me." Keeli looks at the paper and balls it up and drops it in the empty cup holder. " You gonna go see him right!" CiCi asks unable to stay calm.

Keeli starts to rub her temples in hopes that her headache she has gotten from their conversation goes away and fast. "Jayceon, go to school and we will talk about this later."

"Yeah right." CiCi gets out the truck and slams the door in anger and walks off towards the school entrance. Keeli starts her truck up and waits 15 minutes after she has seen him enter the school and finally drives off.

"I was beyond pissed at this point in time. I was having one fucked up morning if I didn't say so myself. First the shit with Juan SUPPOSEDLY helping this bitch move ALL NIGHT LONG. Yeah the fuck right. Aint nobody and I do mean NOBODY moving until no 6 in the morning. That was utter bullshit, and this washed up modeling slut was getting on my fucking nerves. Since the day she waltz her stanking ass into my house I regretted not slumping that bitch at the front door and cooking her body in the woods. This marriage shit was truly making

me a lot more tolerable of bullshit. Because Keeli a few years ago would shot that bitch on sight and yall know it. Put her ass right on outta her misery. But I didn't and now my husband had just cracked the seal on game playing season. Motherfucka had no clue the can of worms he was about to open if he kept playing with me.

Now, on top of that I gotta deal with this Jackie and CiCi bullshit. I never thought this day would come because well, Jackie ass wasn't supposed to be here. His ass was supposed to be rotting out in a cell in some far off land, focusing on keeping his asshole in tact. But instead, thanks to Dumb, and Dumber and STUPID his ass is out here trying his best to make my fucking life miserable. Breathing my air, talking to my child and shit. I was livid just thinking about it. And to know it was my own fucking sister that put this nigga in touch with my baby had me ready to murk everything moving within their lil clique or whatever the fuck they called themselves. Supposed this nigga was tryna do something to harm my son, and her ditzy ass hand delivered her nephew to him. I know you sitting there, rolling your eyes and shit thinking "but that's his father, why would he try and hurt him." Two things that can certainly change people in this world is Jail and Money and now this nigga had experienced them both, so I don't know what kinda shit he was on and wasn't tryna risk my child to find out. I saw pure red as I took off in route to my destination. Here it was I was beefing with the world and it wasn't even 9 fucking A.M as of yet.

I called Donna and told her I would be a little late, but to just let everybody know to sit tight and I was on the way. Getting over there to see Jackie had just become more pressing than getting my peoples back on the street making that gwop. I needed to set his ass straight. I was walking in the door spitting words this go round but if I ever had to see this nigga again, I was coming with a CHOPPA spitting. Nothing else. So it was best he took heed to what I was about to drop in lap this go round."

Keeli pulls into the parking lot of "Jack & Jills" restaurant on Route 1 in College Park Maryland. She hops out the truck and makes her way into the restaurant. Jillian, Jackie's mother is on the cash register working the long line of the breakfast crowd. Keeli walks up to the register and smiles at her in an attempt to not seem as hostile as she really is. Jillian looks up and sees Keeli and smiles a smile a mile long. "Oh my gosh. Look what the wind done blew in."
"Hey Jill. How are you?"
"I'm doing great baby. Hold on one second." Jillian gets one of the girls that is working the serving line to come and take over the register. She walks around to the front

of the counter and gives Keeli a genuinely loving hug. "I can't believe it's you! You look amazing Keeli."

"Thank you. You looking good yourself Jill."

"You want me to get you something to eat?"

"Nah, I just had breakfast not too long ago. Is Jackie here yet?"

"Yes, he's in the back. Have a seat and I'll go get him for you."

"Thanks Jill."

Jillian heads to the back of the restaurant where her office is and Keeli goes and finds an empty table near the huge store front windows and sits down. About 3 minutes later, Jackie emerges from the back office followed by Jillian. Jillian goes back to the cash register and takes over while Jackie walks over to the table where Keeli is sitting and smiles "What's up beautiful?" Jackie asks while taking a seat across from Keeli. "I swear it seems like you get more beautiful as time goes on girl."

"Jackie cut the bullshit. You wanted to see me?"

"Yeah I did."

"You know what, let's talk outside." Keeli stands up and starts heading to the door without another word. Jackie gets up and follows her outside. As they make their way across the parking lot, Jackie can't help but follow the sway of Keeli's ass. He subconsciously grabs his dick and laughs thinking about his sexual past with Keeli. Keeli stops walking when she gets to the rear of her Range Rover.

"You looking real good Ke." Jackie says while eyeing her seductively.

"Fuck all that. I didn't come here to talk about how I look. I came to talk about CiCi."

Jackie leans against Keeli's truck, feeling a tad bit slighted at the way she is responding to him. "Alright, so talk."

"I'ma say this one time, and one time only. I don't know what the fuck you out here tryna pull and frankly, I don't give a shit. You can fuck my sister til you blue in the face. You can spend every dollar she has. You can encourage her to be the biggest motherfucking dope fiend in the history of fiends, I don't care about none of that. But don't you EVER, as long as you live contact my fucking son again Jackie. Or I swear to God on all that is holy, I will put a fucking bullet in your head so quick it's unheard of!

"Damn Keeli." Jackie eyes her with disdain. "YOUR son though?"

"That's right! My goddamn son! Keeli snaps at him with tears of anger in her eyes.

"So what the fuck was you, the virgin Mary or some shit? Last time I checked it was my dick that got your ass pregnant!"

"Yeah and since 1992, I had to be his fucking mother and father!"

"Keeli!" Jackie yells, now completely frustrated. "All that you just said is why I want to be a part of his life. That's my son too. I have fucking rights!"

"Nigga fuck your rights! You gave up your fucking rights when you chose revenge over him! So stay the fuck away from my child and that's the last motherfuckin time I'm gonna say it!"

Jackie laughs at Keeli as he shakes his head in disbelief. He starts to speak to her calm and deliberately. "Keeli, I know you upset right now. So I get you spazzing out and shit. But let us be real here. You and I both know you don't wanna war with me." Jackie takes a few steps closer to her. "Now all these motherfuckas out here in the streets might be scared of you, but you know me baby. And Keeli you KNOW how I gets down."

Keeli takes a step back to put some distance between them. "Well if you come nigga, you better come correct because I'm telling you now if you ever contact my child again, Jill gonna need your fucking dental records to identify your ass now fuck with me." Keeli turns and walks to the driver's side of her truck and gets in and drives off leaving Jackie standing in the middle of the parking lot.

"Apparently, this nigga had no idea who the fuck he was playing with. I wasn't the same little girl who fell in love with him all those years ago.

These days, I was bitch worth more than Bill Gates and was married to a motherfucka with more pull than a game of tug-a-war. The last thing Jackie would want to do is come at me sideways. I could make this nigga disappear like planes in the Bermuda Triangle. He truly had no clue. But to say his threats aint make my skin itch would be a lie. I was irritated as fuck and stewing in anger. SO I decided to go pay a visit to the bitch I felt was sitting at the root of my misery. My little sister.

These smokers had 50 MILLION dollars in cash and a quarter key of coke. Them bitches had to be in heaven at this time. I could not wait to rain on this bitch parade. I knew she was probably sitting over that bitch with a million dollar high and I was gonna blow it for certain."

Keeli parks her truck in CoCo's driveway. She walks up to the large house and rings the doorbell. CoCo's daughter Zalona opens the door and is noticeably sad. She tries to force a smile when she sees Keeli. "Hey Ke."
"What's up. Why you not in school?" Keeli asks while giving her the screw face. "You know what, never mind. Where is your mother?"
"In her fucking crackhouse." Zalona says as she rolls her eyes in disgust.
"Wait a minute. So you know CoCo getting high?"
"Girl please, who don't know. That's all her and Tiff do. You don't know how bad I want to run away every damn day." Zalona states truthfully.
"Zalona, do me a favor. Go wait in my truck for me."
"You gonna let me come stay with you!" Zalona ask with excitement.
"Just go wait in the truck Lona." Keeli hands Zalona her keys and walks past her into the house and Zalona goes out. Keeli closes the front door and walks through the house. She goes downstairs into the basement where she finds CoCo and Tiffany. CoCo is butt naked on her knees performing oral sex on Tiffany who is butt naked and snorting coke off the blade of a butter knife. The lights are low to and the sound system is playing R Kelly's Sex Me. Keeli freezes in shock as she takes in the scene. After she snaps out of shock, pure disgust and rage takes over. Keeli flips on the lights bringing the party to an instant halt. Both girls jump up, naked and embarrassed.
"What you doing here Keeli?" CoCo asks as if she didn't just get caught with a mouth full of pussy.
Keeli runs over and punches Tiffany in her face, knocking her backwards into the glass curio stand. Tiffany and the stand both fall to the floor. "What the fuck you hit her for!" CoCo yells in angers.
"Fuck you! Dyke ass, dopefiend bitch!"

CoCo starts to scream like a mad woman and rushes Keeli. They both fall backwards on the stairs and start

fighting. CoCo bites Keeli's neck like a vampire, after a few hard rights to the side of her face CoCo unlocks her pitbull like grip on her cousin. Keeli pushes CoCo off of her and onto to the floor. They both quickly scramble to their feet. Keeli grabs a lamp off the desk and hits CoCo in her face with it causing it to break and blood to splatter everywhere and CoCo falls back to the floor. Keeli wraps the cord from the lamp around CoCo's neck and starts to choke her with it until she passes out. Keeli unwraps the cord and starts walking towards Tiffany who is finally getting up off the floor crying, with a bloody nose.
"I'm so sorry Ke. I'm so sorry. Please forgive me." Tiffany pleads.
"Bitch I'ma show you sorry!"   Keeli grabs Tiffany by her hair and slings her back down to the floor and begins to beat her viciously with the cord of the broken lamp as Tiffany rolls around on the glass of the broken stand screaming in agony and trying to get away from her enraged sister.   After a full five minutes of viciously beating Tiffany and she is on the verge of passing out, too winded to continue with the torcher, Keeli stops the beating. She stands over top of Tiffany and hog spits in her face. "Bitch if you EVER bring any fucking body around my child again!" Keeli kicks Tiffany in her mouth as hard as she can. She walks over to the coffee table and grabs the ziplock bag of coke and dumps it on Tiffany. She shakes her head in disgust again and then leaves both girls in the basement as she makes her way back upstairs. She walks outside and gets in her truck with Zalona. Zalona smiles knowing what happened just by the way Keeli looks. Zalona sits back in her seat and smiles feeling her mother has gotten what she deserved.

"I was so through with them stankin bitches in the basement it aint make no kinds of sense. Tiffany was my sister, and I loved

her. I loved CoCo too which is why although I wanted to kill them I didn't. I was gonna look into getting Tiff some help, but until she got it wasn't shit she could say to me ever in life. After the morning I had been having I really just wanted to go home and crawl back in my fucking bed and start over. But I couldn't. I had more pressing issues to deal with. My team was waiting on me and I still had to go and help Ciaira out. And to top it off, I now had to figure out what the hell I was gonna do with Zalona.

I went and met with the team first and to say everybody was eager to get back to work was an understatement. I let them know we would officially be open for business again in 2 weeks and the only changes were the captains were gonna be in charge of holding on to their crews supply for the whole month. I didn't like it too much because it left a huge window for error BUT at the same time, I didn't have anywhere to store that shit any longer. Them bitches sold the warehouse which was so stupid. And since I wasn't supposed to be dealing with this shit directly anymore per me and Juan's agreement, I had to keep my hands touching the shit to a minimum. After I made sure they understood the new rules of engagement, and how they were 100 percent responsible for whatever they touched. I didn't want to hear shit about stick up boys, police or none of that shit. I hadn't made it this far in the game by giving many fucks and playing many games, so I wasn't about to start now. Next order of business was the new cell phones. Yeah, pagers were dying out, so we had to step it up. All my capos needed to have what we came to call burner phones. 30 days and toss that shit. They were prepaid so no information had to be given. I was footing the bill for them each month. So when you get your new one, I take the old one to make sure that shit gets destroyed. The phones were strictly for business. Not for calling baby mothers and fathers, ordering pizzas, or giving as your childs emergency contact at school. The only person they were supposed to call from them shits was me and it had to be for one of two reasons. They had my money or somebody was DEAD. Point Blank. All that other shit, wait til you see a motherfucka.

After I finished up with them, me and Zalona went over to help Ciaira out at the shop. When I saw how extensive the damage was to her shit I was speechless, and heartbroken for my girl. This was her dream and she put so much into making it happen, now some bitch or bitch ass nigga was tryna stop her shine. That made me livid. And the fact that we didn't know who was playing these games pissed me off even more. But one thing for sure was whoever did this shit had a personal vendetta against Ciaira. Wasn't nothing at all random about the amount of damage these motherfuckas caused. I was stuck trying to figure out who would want to bring Ciaira grief. She was one of the sweetest bitches ever....unless you got her wrong, but as far as I knew nobody had gotten her wrong in a minute.

We worked trying our best to clean up what we could until about 8:30 that night. When we left I was exhausted and decided that Zalona was just gonna have to stay with me for a minute until I sorted this shit out. I was too tired to blink, let alone cook so I stopped at KFC and grabbed some chicken on the way in. I planned to feed the kids, eat, take a bubble bath and sleep. I wasn't even getting up and taking the kids to school the next day. Juan ass didn't know it yet but he was officially on duty. I was plotting on sleeping til noon the next day at a minimum. But I had no idea pulling up into my driveway that little shit I had just dealt with today would hold no barring on the drama set to unfold the moment I crossed the threshold. I could've sworn my welcome mat changed to read "Welcome to the Major League of problems".

Keeli and Zalona get out the truck, grab the food from the backseat and start heading to the house. "Ke, you sure Juan aint gonna trip about me staying here?" Zalona asks nervously.
"Girl hush, aint nobody thinking about Juan ass. Come on." Keeli uses her keys to unlock and open the door and they both walk into the house. "I'm home!" Keeli announces loudly from the foyer.
"For a house full of kids, it sure is quiet in here."
"Yeah, too damn quiet." Keeli quickly walks into the family room as the start of her search for her family. She stops in her tracks when she finds Ishmel, Mecca and Asha snuggled up on the sectional under a large blanket asleep. There are a bunch of snack sized potato chip bags, empty juice boxes and crumbs on the floor. On the coffee table is a half loaf of bread, an empty jar of peanut butter and an empty jelly jar. Next to it is two half eaten sandwiches and a bunch of bite size snickers wrappers. Keeli goes over and starts to wake the kids who all have sticky faces and hands. "What the hell were y'all doing?
"We were hungry mommy, so we made sandwiches" Mecca answers truthfully and innocently.
"Where is CiCi and why the hell did he let y'all sit and eat all this shit!" Keeli asks in frustration.
"He's not here." Ishmel informs her.
"What you mean here not here?"
"He left right after daddy did."
"I don't feel good mommy. My tummy hurts." Asha begins to whine.
Keeli picks up her daughter and hugs her as she rest her head on her shoulder. "Zalona, take that food in the kitchen for me please. Y'all come on upstairs so I can get y'all cleaned up and ready for bed."

Keeli and the kids head upstairs while Zalona takes the food into the kitchenand fixes herself a plate. After Keeli gives the kids pepto chewables to helpwith their stomach aches, she cleans them up and puts them to bed. Once she has them settled, she goes into the master bedroom and sits down on her chaise and grabs the phone. She calls Juan on his cellphone. With every passing ring, she grows a little more angry about the situation. Finally after the 5th ring, Juan answers the phone. Keeli grows angrier because she can hear the latin music blaring in the background and he is laughing a full 60 seconds before he finally speaks into the phone.

"What's up Mami."
"Where the fuck are you?" Keeli snaps, unable to pretend with Juan at this point.
"Why? What's up?"
"Why what's up?" Keeli repeats the question in disbelief as she moves the phone away from her ear and looks at it as if it's a foreign object. She puts the phone back to her hear and snaps. "What's up is my motherfucking babies been in this bitch by themselves all goddamn day! That's what's up!"
"What? I'm on my way right now!"
"Don't bother." Keeli hangs up the phone even more pissed than when she first picked it up. She goes back downstairs and begins to clean up the mess the kids created. Once she is done she joins Zalona in the kitchen where they sit, eat and talk. Just as Keeli starts to wash the dishes, Juan comes rushing into the house with urgency. He starts calling her name as he makes his way from room to room until he finds her in the kitchen.
"Man what the hell is going on around here?"
"Aint shit." Keeli says sarcastically. "Just my babies was up in here by themselves all evening while you were out doing whatever you was doing. But I'm sure it was of OOBER importance, so fuck their safety. It's all good."
"Where is CiCi?"
"I don't know Juan. According to my children with stomach aches from all the junk they ate because they were hungry and nobody was here to feed then, CiCi left right after you did."

"You call his cell baby?" Juan asks in a loving tone in hopes that the sarcasm stops.

"No I didn't. I took his cell from him this morning."

"Why you do that?"

"I have my reasons." Keeli responds, not wanting to tell Juan everything for fear of a different fight taking place.

"Why didn't you stay here with them?"

"Cause he's damn near 15 years old Keeli. He don't need no babysitter. Or at least I didn't THINK his ass did."

"I swear to God I'm gonna kill him. His little stankin ass is so dead the minute he walk through this door tonight." Keeli looks at Juan with confusion all over her face. "And where is Ti?"

"Oh, she spending the rest of the week with her mother. I'm gonna go pick her up Sunday."

"So she just gonna be outta school until Monday huh. That's what's up." Keeli states sarcastically as she walks away from Juan feeling some kinda way about HER family spending so much time with Maranda. Juan walks up behinds her and pulls her into his embrace.

"Bae, just stop stressing. Right now let's just concentrate on finding CiCi. Come on, we will go out and look for him."

Keeli looks at Zalona. "Lona, if he gets back here before we do, just tell him I went to the store then go in another room and call me ASAP."

"Ok" Zalona answers as Keeli and Juan leave the kitchen and she goes over to the sink to finish washing the dishes Keeli had started.

"Me and Juan left on a hunt for this big head ass child of mine. I didn't know which one of them I was more pissed with at this point but I did know I was 100% pissed. It's crazy how Juan beat the hell out of me

thinking that I would get back down to DC, switch up and he would lose me.... Now here I was watching everybody from my husband to my fucking kids switch up and I was the one losing them. I wanted to just ride by myself to look for CiCi, but Juan insisted we ride together. I had fought enough for one day so I didn't even protest. Just got in the Benz and rode with him.

We checked the community center, basketball court, the school, the gas station. Any and every where these suburban gangstas CiCi ran with dwelled is where we checked, and my baby was nowhere to be found. I started to quickly go from feeling mad at him for rolling out on his siblings to worrying about if something had happened to my child. I would never forgive myself if it did.

We got back home a little after 11 and he still wasn't there. I had been wearing a brave face for over the last hour while inside I was consumed with worry, but by the time I crossed that threshold again I couldn't hold back my tears. It felt like someone was choking the life out of me as I sat on the sofa in my family room and held no control over the tears that escaped my eyes. I just kept thinking if something happened to him. What if Jackie had done something to my child. The only other time I had been this afraid was when Bell and his people held my entire family hostage over bullshit. They all walked away unscathed but it still cost his ass his life. If something happened to CiCi I swore before God right then it was gonna cost SO many motherfuckas their lives. Starting with the nigga I said I DO to, cause had the fuck he been home like he was supposed to CiCi ass would still be here.

Around midnight I grabbed the phone and called the police. That was not a Keeli Byrd, Queen of DC move, That was a Keeli Byrd, mother of Jayceon Green move. I had never called on the police before in life and now I knew why. They wasn't about shit. They told me he had to be missing at minimum 24 hours before they would make a report. I almost lost it. In 24 hours my child could be dismembered and buried, when for all we knew he could be walking pass a police officer RIGHT NOW but they would never know he was missing because of some stupid ass 24 hour rule. I didn't even want to think about the number of children, women, hell even men who probably were never seen again because their love one had to wait an entire 24 hours from the time they were last seen by them to report them missing.

Police wasn't about shit.

Juan seeing me grow more and more angry by the second after that phone call to my local police department got CiCi cell from me and started to call all his friends. Nobody gave a fuck that it was after midnight and these people should have been asleep. My child was missing and my heart was fearing the worst...

That I had lost him.

Of course all his little stupid ass friends we were able to reach were claiming that hadn't been in touch with him, but we knew how kids lied for each other. Me and Ciaira used to do that shit all the time. Around 1am, Zalona went to bed and me and Juan waited....

And waited.

And waited.

And waited some more.

I grabbed the phone and begin to call our family and friends, again not giving two fucks about the time, but it was to no avail because nobody had seen CiCi. I finally broke down and called one of the last people on earth I wanted to speak to. I hated Jackie, and wished he fucking just went away but if he knew where our child was I needed to know. Or if he had anything to do with him being missing. I know it sound harsh but I already told you I did not trust this motherfucka anymore. Jackie had been gone too many years to still be the same. Too much in this world had changed. Motherfuckas these days took out their own family on a regular basis in this game.

Remember Aunt Rita?

So nah, I wasn't giving him no fucking father pass. Until I laid eyes on my child everybody and their fucking daddy was a suspect including his own.

Jackie said he hadn't seen or heard from him since the day before and then started grilling me because I was the custodial parent. You could hear in his voice that he was genuinely concerned and he promised if he heard anything from CiCi or he showed up there he would call me immediately.

Around 4am I was at my lowest point and couldn't think of anything other than my child being in a ditch somewhere hurt and dying and me not being able to save him. I literally felt like the life was being sucked from my body, and just when I thought I would die from the pain of losing my baby.....

THIS LITTLE MOTHERFUCKA CAME WALTZING IN THE DOOR!"

CiCi walks into the foyer and turns around and locks the door. Keeli and Juan run out the kitchen and down the hall when they hear the door close. She stops in her tracks and a smile a mile wide spreads across her face as she runs to CiCi and embraces him as tightly as possible. Keeli begins to sway back and forth as she hugs her first born child and tears of a mother's love begin to fall down her face.

"Oh my God CiCi. Please tell me you are okay. I was worried sick about you. Are you okay baby?" Keeli rambles.
"Yeah man." CiCi snaps as he tries to pull away from Keeli's grip.
"What happened to you baby. Where were you?"
"Nothing man. Aint nothing happen to me and I wasn't no where now can you get off me?"
Keeli takes a step back and looks up at CiCi sideways. His eyes are extremely low and it finally registers to her that he reeks of marijuana and alcohol. "What did you just say to me?" Keeli asks for clarity, trying to convince herself that something must be wrong with her ears.
"I said can you get off me." CiCi responds in a challenging tone.
Keeli shakes her head and disbelief. "Have you been smoking Jayceon?"
"Man, fuck outta here. You blowing me." CiCi says as he waves Keeli and her line of questioning off. He attempts to walk away but before he can make a complete turn Keeli hauls off and smacks the fuck outta him. "WHO THE FUCK DO YOU THINK YOU TALKING TO! DO YOU FUCKING REALIZE I'VE BEEN RUNNING AROUND THIS BITCH ALL NIGHT LOOKING FOR YOUR LITTLE STUPID

144

ASS!"

"WHO THE FUCK ASKED YOU TOO!" CiCi yells, the boom in his voice registering just a few octaves louder than hers. "I don't need you to be out looking for me or worrying about me. Focus on your husband or your step daughter or one of them fucking brats upstairs but I'm good. They fucking need you. I DON'T."

Keeli stands there rubbing her temples in disbelief. She takes a deep breath to calm herself before she begins to speak. "Jayceon, it's 4 in the morning. You fucked up and obviously tripping. So I'mma give youa pass. Go ahead upstairs and get some sleep and we will deal with whatever it is that is bothering you in the morning."

"Whatever." CiCi mugs Keeli as he walks away from her and past Juan who is sitting on the stairs watching the whole scene unfold. He takes to the stairs two at a time and goes upstairs in his room and slams the door.

Keeli finally takes a breath after being stuck at her son's display of disrespect for her. She walks over to the stairs and takes a seat beside Juan as the tears begin to roll down her face with no regard for her gangsta. She looks up at Juan with eyes filled with hurt and confusion. "Why you aint say nothing babe?"

"Because I'm not his father. And if he had started popping all that gangsta shit with me, I would've split his shit no question. Then you and I would have had a problem and I don't want that.

"What I'mma do with him baby. He only fucking 14 and he carrying on like this."

"Go get in the bed Keeli. I'mma go up and talk to him."

"No that's ok. I'm gonna go and set his ass straight right now cause if I don't it will only get worse and I'm not even about to be disrespected and disregarding by any fucking child I gave birth to."

"You sure you wanna do this now boo?"

"I don't wan't to do this shit ever. But I got to if I ever want my son to respect me past this moment in time."

"Alright. Let me know if you need me."

Keeli stands up and closes her eyes and says a quick and silently prayer. She walks up the stairs and goes to CiCi's bedroom and walks in. He is sitting on the edge of his King Sized bed talking to someone on the phone. He looks at Keeli and blows her off as he continues his conversation. "Hang up the phone." Keeli demands. "You don't know how to knock?" CiCi bucks as he turns his back to her. Keeli, now officially over his disrespect walks over to the phone cord and yanks it out the wall disconnecting his call instantly. CiCi throws the phone down and jumps up in Keeli's face. "What the fuck you do that for!"
"Because it's four in the fucking morning and further I'm your mother and this is my motherfuciing house!"
"So what bitch!" CiCi spat, officially over the edge.
Keeli slaps CiCi as hard as humanly possible causing his face to feel as though it is on fire from the inside out. Having officially lost her cool, Keeli jumps on CiCi and starts attacking him. CiCi, at this point being taller than his mother grabs Keeli by her waist and lifts her into the air and slams her on his bed in a wresting type move. Juan who has been standing at the door watching the entire exchange go down finally moves into the room and quickly yanks CiCi off of Keeli by his shirt and slams him into the wall. He then wraps his hands around CiCi's neck and begins to choke the life out of him.

"Motherfucka if you EVER put your fucking hands on my wife again I'll fucking kill you!"
Keeli rushes over and grabs Juan as she sees life looking as though it isofficially fleeing CiCi's body. "Baby let him go please."
"Nah fuck that. I gave you a chance to handle it but apparently he think he your fucking father or something." Juan refocuses his attention on CiCI. "I don't know what the fuck your problem is and I frankly don't care but as

long as I'm around you gonna fucking respect her even
                              when the fuck you don't
                              want to!
"Baby please let him go. He turning purple. PLEASE
JUAN!" Keeli cries out as her tears continue to fall. Juan
lets go of CiCi and his body melts to the floor as he begins
to cough uncontrollably. "You heard me nigga!" Juan
yells while standing over top of a heaving CiCi.
"Yeah man." CiCi manages to get out between his dry
heaving.
Juan grabs him by his shirt and yanks him up off the
floor. "Fuck that, you address me as sir you disrespectful
little piece of shit! And you fucking apologize to your
mother NOW!
CiCi looks at Keeli with eyes filled with humiliation and
hurt and mumbles. "I'm sorry ma."
"She can't fucking hear you. Say that shit louder!" Juan
demands.
"It's okay Papi. Just let him go please."
"You sure? Cause I aint got no qualms about fucking his
little punk ass up right here." Juan says while looking CiCi
in the eyes letting him know he would kill him without a
second thought if his wife gave the word.
"Yes Papi. It's ok. Just give us a minute please."
Juan lets go of CiCi's shirt and lets him drop back to the
floor. "I'mma go in the room and you gonna sit here and
listen to what the fuck she got to say.And I swear to God
if I hear anything different I'm coming back and I can
promise you as much as I love your mother not even she
will be able to stop me from putting a fucking bullet in
your head. You got me."
"Yes sir." CiCi says while looking down at his feet.
Juan walks out the bedroom door and closes it behind
him.
"CiCi listen......." Keeli begins in an attempt to try and fix
things between her and her son.
"I didn't mean it." CiCi says calmly as the tears he's been
trying to hold back begin to fall.

"Baby I know. You high right now and ......"
"No." CiCi chuckles. "I'm saying I didn't mean it when I apologized." He looks up at Keeli and his eyes are filled with hate, anger and confusion. "You and your husband can beat on me. Y'all can punish me. Y'all can do whatever but it aint gonna work. It aint gonna change nothing. I hate you so much Keeli. I literally pray for the day both of y'all fucking die or go to jail so I can go and live with my fucking father."
Keeli looks at her first born child with constant tears running down her face.
"You mean that don't you?"
"I said it didn't" CiCi snaps, mocking Juan's famous line.
"CiCi you don't even know him. You've talked to his ass what once since you were two years old."
"So what! The only reason he wasn't around is because he was in jail. What the fuck is your excuse."
"Excuse me?" Keeli asks incredulously. The last time I checked I was the one that has been here day in and day out since the day your ass was born CiCi."
"Yeah you WAS there. I will give you that. You WAS there until you got your little fake ass cartel up and running."
"CiCi what the hell are you talking about? You tripping."
"Nah you tripping if you think for one fucking second I don't know what's up."
"CiCi I really don't know what you talking about. You high as shit right now and I guess hallucinating or some shit." Keeli attempts to wave off the accusations.
CiCi goes over and sits on his bed and starts laughing.
"You really think I'm stupid don't you. You think I don't know what you and Ciaira been doing all these years. Why I always had to be at Grandma house and shit. Why we got way more money and bullshit that we fucking need."
Keeli sits down on the bed beside CiCi and takes a deep breath as she prepares to clear her conscious. "You right

CiCi. I sold drugs. Did it for years. When your father
went to jail
he left me out here in these streets with nothing but YOU.
There was days we didn't even have food to eat, so yes I
got the fuck on my grind and did what I had to do support
you, me, your aunts, your uncle,
your grandmother hell even your great grandmother. I did
that shit back then, but CiCi I don't get down anymore. I
did that shit back then so you would never have to."
"Yeah." CiCi laughs. "You keep telling yourself that shit
Keeli."
"It's the fucking truth!" Keeli yells at him. "Every fucking
Key I copped and every ounce I sold was for your ass,
and then for you and your brothers!"
"I aint never ask for NONE of this bullshit Keeli. I aint ask
for no fucking Mansion on Long Island. I aint ask for no
summer home in Miami. I aint ask for NONE of this
fucking bullshit! The only thing I wanted and needed was
you ma! But you was always too fucking busy. I wanted
your time but all you ever offered me was your bullshit!
"That's bullshit CiCi and you know it!" Keeli yells through
her tears as the guilt of what her son is accusing her of
starts to eat at her heart.
"The only reason you called yourself stopping or whatever
is because you had Asha and married Juan. But the crazy
shit is you still aint never home. Now you too busy with
clothing lines, real estate and all that other fake legal
bullshit.
"CiCi." Keeli pauses, unsure of what she wants to say at
this point. "Baby it's just complicated to explain but..."
"Look, why don't you do us all a favor and let me go and
stay with my father. He got time for me."
"If he got so much fucking time for you, why the fuck he
aint been here for the past fucking decade and change
CiCi!" Keeli yells, completely hurt and no longer able to
put up a brave front.
CiCi looks at her and smiles as he goes in for the kill. "He
was away

because he had to be. You was away because you CHOSE to be Keeli." Keeli sits frozen on his bed as his words echo in her brain causing the knife to go deeper into her heart. "Since you quiet now, I guess you finished your little speech and shit. So can you get the fuck outta my room so I can get some sleep now.

Keeli walks out of the room with tears pouring from her eyes. She leans against the wall in the hallway and lets the pain in her heart escape through her eyes. Juan comes up to her and hugs her and she buries her face into his chest and cries uncontrollably.

"He hates me baby."

"No he doesn't Keeli. Just calms down."

"Yes he does. He said he hates me and wishes I either die or go to jail so he can go and live with Jackie. I put my fucking life on the line so he could have a better one and he hates me."

Juan takes a deep breath in an attempt to control his building anger. "Go lay down baby."

"I can't." Keeli cries sounding more and more pitiful by the second.

"Just go lay down. I'ma talk to him and straighten this out."

"Okay. Thanks baby." Keeli wipes her eyes as she walks down the hall into the master suite. She lays on the bed and silently cries as CiCi's words continuously play in her head. Down the hall, Juan stands outside CiCi's bedroom door trying to calm himself before he goes to talk with him. CiCi gets undressed and climbs into his huge bed and pulls the covers over his head and attempts to finally get some sleep. Juan walks into his room and over to the bed and snatches him out the bed by his arm. CiCi falls to the floor and jumps up shocked.

"Get your shit on! You wanna leave, lets go!" Juan shouts.

"Huh? What you talking about?" CiCi asks in confusion.
"You wanna go stay with your bitch ass father, lets go! I aint studder."
"Man….." CiCi begins to protest and Juan grabs him and presses him to the wall.
"I said lets go nigga! That shit aint up for discussion."
"Alright man, let me get my stuff."
"You aint paid for shit in here slim. All this shit was brought with drug money so you cool on that. Put the shit you had on today back on and then get the fuck outta my house."
"Man, Juan listen……."
"Fuck all that you talking. Let's go!" Juan pushes CiCi out the bedroom into the hallway and he lands on the floor. Juan grabs his clothes off the chair in his room that he had on that day, along with his coat and shoes and throws the stuff on top of him. "Get dressed nigga!"
CiCi stands up and begins to put his clothes on as Keeli comes out the master suite. "What the hell are you doing Juan?"
"His ass wanna go, he gone!"
"Juan please…." Keeli attempts to reason with him.
"Shut the fuck up! This nigga think he big and he feeling himself talking about where the fuck he wanna go, so his ass going and that's that!" Juan grabs CiCi by his arm and drags him down the stairs as Keeli runs behind them. Juan opens the front door and pushes CiCi outside and slams it in his face. Keeli runs to the door and tries to open it and Juan pushes her back. "If you open that door, I swear to God Keeli."
"It's fucking five in the morning and cold as hell out there."
"So what!" Juan grabs Keeli by the arm and leads her back upstairs to their master suite. He closes and locks the door. "Go to sleep or something. Look at you, all \stressed out. Crying and shit over his little ungrateful ass!"

"He's my baby Juan! I'm supposed to be worried about
                        him! That's my job as his
                        mother!"
"First he aint no fucking baby! He's you son! You got 3
fucking babies down the hall that need you! How the fuck
you gonna be there for them, when you giving all your
energy to him and all his dumb shit!" Keeli sucks her
teeth and heads toward the door. "Oh so what you don't
care about them Keeli?"
Keeli looks at Juan in disbelief. "Of course I care about
them! Those are my babies! I love ALL our kids with
everything I fucking am! But you acting like
I'm not supposed to care about CiCi and what happens to
him and that's some bullshit Juan."
"Come here Keeli." Juan says while patting his thigh.
Keeli walks over and sits on his lap as the tears start to
fall again. "I'm never saying you not supposed to love or
care about CiCi. He's your first born, so you gonna love
his ass no matter what. Shit, I love him. I don't see him
as my step son. I've always seen him as my SON and you
know that. You don't think it hurt me to have to put his
ass out?
"So you saying you would do the same thing to Mecca and
Ish?"
"No. I'd do worse to them. I would've beat the living shit
outta them first if they ever spoke to you like that or
pulled the shit he pulled today. THEN I would've threw
their ass out. But see, even though I love CiCi like he
mines, at the end of the day he's not. So while I wanted
to break his shit, I couldn't. Look, just give him a few
days. Let him go ahead and be over there with that
nigga. Once he see shit aint sweet, he gonna check his
bullshit and come home."
"You sure."
"Trust me. CiCi been hanging off your tiddy for far too
long to give it up cold turkey. Now come on and lay
down. Lets get some sleep.

152

"Nah, I might as well go on and stay up. It's already after
                    5 and I gotta get the kids up
                    in a little bit."
"I want you to chill today. Stay in bed and get some rest.
I'll take the brats to school and get my mother to pick
them up. They can stay over there tonight."
"Well I still gotta get up because I gotta help Ciaira with
some stuff."
"Not today you don't, You chilling Ke."
"So what about Zalona?"
"I'll take her to your mother's house when I take the kids
to school." Juan gets up and undresses Keeli and then
helps her into their huge bed and
tucks her in.
"So what about you? You been up all night too and......"
"Baby relax. As soon as I drop them off I'll be right back.
We aint gonna do nothing but sleep all day. Now go
ahead and get started, I'ma go make them breaksfast."
Keeli blushes as she gets comfortable under the covers. "I
love you Papi."
"I love you too Mami." Juan kisses Keeli on the forehead
and leaves the room.

**_"At this point, I was too damn tired to sleep.
I just laid there with the covers pulled up to
my neck staring at the TV. I couldn't get
over how shit went down with CiCi. I put
my life on the line for him day in and day
out. I gave this child ANYTHING he asked
for and boatloads of shit he didn't, yet in his
mind, I wasn't there for him._**

**_In hindsight, I can admit that I could have
spent more time with CiCi coming up. But_**

what he seems to not understand is it aint like I was rolling like a lot of bitches I know. Where he was getting left with Grandma so I can go shake my ass with Rare Essence or no shit like that. I was a single mother with the responsibility of making sure me, him, my siblings and hell even my own fucking mother survived. If I had sat on my ass and played the cards I was dealt, right now CiCi would be hating me for a whole different list of reasons. It would be along the same list of reasons I hated my mother for so damn long behind. All the times I saw our little bit of shit sat out in the street before I decided to get it how I live, yeah that shit does something to a child's spirit. And I REFUSED to let mine go through that but yet and still I'm the bad guy, and the nigga who decided because he was behind the wall, he couldn't even do as much as pick up a phone or put pen to paper for the sake of our son..... he's a hero. To say I was livid was an understatement. But like Juan said, I had 3 more children who needed me and in the shape CiCi had me in, I was no good to nobody so I had to pull it together ASAP.

I finally relaxed and let the sleep my body was fighting for take hold of me. Around 10am, the phone started ringing off the hook. I jumped up out of my sleep and my heart and mind instantly started racing. All my thoughts went to CiCi and I immediately

thought the worst. I glared at that ringing phone and said a silent prayer before I picked it up because God knows as much as I loved Juan, if something had happened to CiCi I was gonna kill his ass LITERALLY and wasn't no two ways about that shit."

Keeli grabs the phone and takes a deep breath before speaking. "Hello."
Ciaira sniffles into the phone trying to stop her tears. "
Are you up?"
"Yeah. What's wrong with you? Are you crying Ciaira?"
"Just come open the door."
"Alright here I come."

Keeli gets out the bed and grabs her robe and slippers and puts them on and heads out the room. She comes downstairs and opens the door. Ciaira ushers her two children Byron and Rasheeda into the house and comes in behind them. Keeli closes the door.

"What's going on?"
"Byron, take your sister upstairs while I talk to aunt Ke."
"Okay ma. Come on Sheeda." Byron says as he grabs his sister hand and leads her up the stairs. Keeli walks down the hall into the kitchen and Ciaira follows her.
"You wanna know what's goping on? This is what's going on!" Ciaira takes off her sunglasses and her right eye is swollen shut and three different shades of purple.
'What the fuck happened to you!"
"That bitch hit me!"
"Who! What the fuck!"
"ROC! The bitch got busted and he hit me. So I stabbed his motherfucking ass!"

"What the fuck is going on?" Keeli asks while rubbing her temples and trying to make sense of what she is hearing. "Yeah, his bitch called me last night and told it all. I confronted him this morning and the bitch couldn't take the heat. So he hit me and I started slicing cause I'm not even about to play that bullshit and you know it."

"Trust me, I know you not." Keeli sits down at the table and Ciaira sits across from her and tears start to fall.

"The bitch said her name Niyah"

"Hold up, Niyah? You sure?"

"Yeah. What you know her or something?" Ciaira questions.

"The bitch from the boat ride that night that Monae came home."

"I remember that night but I don't remember no bitch. But anyway, she called my motherfucking house talking about her and Roc this, and her and Roc that. I might as well get my brats and roll cause she four months pregnant."

"Whoa whoa wait! How the fuck she four months and we only been back down this bitch for two months."

"Oh honey listen cause it only get better. According to her, all them business trips them niggas was making down here when we was upstate wasn't all business ya know."

"Them niggas?" Keeli asks, trying to make sure she's hearing Ciaira correctly.

"Yes honey. THEM NIGGAS."

"I don't need this shit today with all I got going on with CiCi."

"What's wrong with CiCi?"

"So much shit, I don't even feel like reliving it through conversation at the moment. We on you now. Y'all gonna stay here and we will deal with all this shit. Let's start with getting you something for that eye."

Keeli starts walking to the freezer when the phone starts ringing, She grabs it and answers on the second ring. "Hello"

"Hey, It's Jack. I was calling to let you know CiCi here with me and he's fine." Jackie informs her.
Keeli perks up a bit. "Can I speak to him?"
"Nah, he chilling right now Ke. Tryna get his mind right."
"Why are you trying to take my baby from me Jackie?: Keeli asks as her eyes begin to fill up with tears.
"Aint nobody tryna take him from you Keeli. I just wanna get to know my son and that's all. So chill out please. Look, although you came at me foul as fuck, I can understand your hesitation and I honestly appreciate how much you care about CiCi. He all I got out here and I just wanna try and build with my son. I promise I will call you every day to let you know how he doing until y'all stop beefing. Is that fair?
"Yes, that's fair. And thank you. I appreciate it."
"No problem. I told you I don't want no problems Keeli."
"Thank you Jackie." Keeli smiles.
"No problem."
"Oh and Jackie, call me on my cell so it wont be no problems."
"I got you. I just ask that you do the same."
"No problem." Keeli laughs. "Take care of my baby Jackie."
"I will Keeli. I promise I wont let you down."
"Ok. And tell CiCi I love him."
"I will."

Keeli hangs up the phone and wipes the tears out of her eyes.

"Maybe I was overreacting about CiCi spending time with Jackie. He didn't HAVE to call me, but he did and I appreciated it. His phone call removed a bit of the stress from my brain and gave me the space to

deal with this shit Ciaira had just thrown in my lap.

While Ciaira was my ace, she was a big girl and could handle her own affairs. My mind was focused on one statement in our whole conversation....... THEM NIGGAS. So now my question became, "Is Juan cheating?" That's what I really needed to know immediately. I was wise enough to know that just coming out and asking him wasn't gonna get me the info I needed. All that would do was put his ass on notice that my ass was on notice and cause him to bury his shit deeper. I couldn't have that. While I loved Juan, he was just like any other nigga with a dick swinging between his legs. Dana always told me never give a nigga a heads up, give his ass just enough rope to hang himself. So that's what I was gonna do to find out what was REALLY good.

That night, Roc came over to plead his case but Ciaira wasn't having that shit and they ended up having this big huge screaming match in the middle of my family room. Roc kept tryna convince Ciaira that the sky was purple with yellow polka dots by swearing the chick was telling all lies. And Ciaira kept tryna get him to just kiss her ass and accept that they were done. Once he finally realized all his yelling was in vain..... and his pride was butt hurt he finally left.

Ciaira and the kids stayed...

FOR TWO FUCKING MONTHS!!!!!!!!

Shit was 100 % crazy. It felt like fucking kids was everywhere. I couldn't fucking fart in peace. Then me and Juan started beefing something awful. He showed his true colors because all that "sis" shit between him and Ciaira went out the window the minute she kicked his peoples to the curb. So he wanted her gone, because yes Roc wanted her gone, but the both had me fucked up. Ciaira was my family. I had did her dirty before and although it had been many moons since me and her had that shouting match in Simm living room, there were times the guilt of that shit would pop up and tap me on the shoulder. My girl had been through a lot so she was more than welcome to stay while she cleared her head and figured out her next move..... and she did.

CiCi was doing fine. He had finally started to call me since he had been with Jackie. I knew he missed me and well of course I missed my damn baby, but he was proving himself as a man I guess so I let the shit play out. Jackie still called me once a day to fill me in on our son and I greatly appreciated that. Zalona was back in Philly with my Grandma Vickey because well her deadbeat ass mother never even fucking picked up the phone to try and find her child. That bitch head was soooooo deep in snort at this point it was pathetic. Jackie told me them bitches were 100 % done. He stopped short of telling me how him and Simm were working the strings on their asses but his silence spoke volumes. I personally didn't give a fuck. As long as CiCi was straight and Jackie was being honorable with my son I couldn't lend two fucks to my sister and cousin at this point in their pathetic little lives.

So that was the jist of shit for the most part so while I was trying to continue to be everything, I was stressed. And every now and again, I thought about the fact that me and Ciaira STILL had not made it to see BJ. I felt like shit for that considering all my man had done for me. Shit I wanted to see him every day BUT life just wasn't permitting that shit right now and from the look of things it would be awhile before we were able to hit the highway in the name of BJ.

FINALLY, Ciaira and the kids moved out and yes while I loved her, Byron and Rasheeda, I sung Jesus praises as I helped my girl carry their shit through their own front door. She brought a 3 bedroom house out in Kensington, Maryland so we were still fairly close to each other. Me and her also went in together and brought a three story building on H Street NE. We were turning it into a boutique that would carry her clothing line "Bubbles" and mine "QYH/KYH" (Queen of Your Hood/ King of Your Hood). We each would have our own floors and the third floor was going to be a "Byrd's Books". We were so excited about our new business venture. Remodeling started 2 weeks after we brought the spot and we had the grand opening set for the upcoming spring.

When Ciaira brought a house, Roc finally accepted that she was done with his ass SO this dumb ass nigga decided the best possible solution to it all was to move this Niyah bitch in with him. And true enough, she was 6 months pregnant. Was it Roc's kid..... I couldn't tell ya BUT he was damn sure rocking as if it was. Ciaira was hurt, but she held her head high and simply said FUCK THAT NIGGA then she threw his ass 500,000 and officially brought him out of "Bubbles." I was proud of my girl cause man I don't know if I could've been so G where my heart was concerned. But she put her big girl drawls on and worked out visitation with him for Rasheeda and financial support WITHOUT the courts getting involved. She knew that left her open to getting burned by his ass again but running to the court building and police station had never been our thing. We handled shit. And that's what my girl did.

Now when Ciaira and her kids flew the nest I thought the strain between me and Juan would be over with. Boy oh boy was I wrong. It felt like shit got worse instantly. This mofo was missing in action ALL the time. Staying out all night which he knew was some shit I didn't even play. Me and him stayed arguing about anything and everything. Shit was just sick.

Since the boutique wasn't scheduled to open til April and QDC productions wasn't gonna open until June, I decided to take the rest of the year "off". I decided to just spend time being a mommy and working on my book. I wanted it to be finished by my birthday because in June it would be the first book released by QDC Productions. I prayed things would get better between me and my husband and in the meantime I just worked hard to reach my goals. Then in January, something happened that left me stuck on stupid. They say Karma wasn't shit to play with and when you do people dirty.... It comes back to bite you in the ass and the bite is ALWAYS hard to recover from, and I was about to see that shit first hand."

"Emotional"

January 2004

"This was the first holiday season since I had been getting money that I was GLAD to see go. I used to live for this time of year but not this go round. Since Thanksgiving, well hell even before then shit had been fucked up. I was living out the lyrics to "There's A Stranger in My House." and that shit was NOT OK.

On Thanksgiving, we were supposed to go to Sissy's for dinner but then me and Juan got into this HUGE argument about absolutely NOTHING. He took the kids and went on and I stayed home alone. My family was in Philly and Ciaira and her kids went down south to be with her family. So my Thanksgiving was fucked up and lonely as hell.

Then baby Jesus birthday was the straw that broke the camel's back. We, meaning me and my husband and our kids had planned to spend Christmas in Miami. We planned this back in September and everything was set in stone and ready. Well on December 22nd, the day we were scheduled to leave Juan informs me that he aint going. Said with the same emotion as "We outta milk." He said TiTi wanted to be with her mother because this was their first Christmas together since 1993. I understood that just a little but then when he told me that Sissy wants him home for Christmas so he aint going I was like Nigga fuck you too.

That night me and my kids, my mother and siblings boarded my plane and flew to Miami to continue with our holiday as planned. I even reached out and invited my dad, step mother and brother down to spend Christmas with us because it had been quite some time. My dad opted not to come and wouldn't allow my brother to come either. By now, everyone knew of Tiff's condition and well my father blamed me. In his eyes, I held her crack pipe to her lips for her each and every time she got high. So fuck him too was how I was carrying shit. Ciaira and her kids came down the day after Christmas and we had a ball. We all left and went home the day after New Years.

When we got back, CiCi went back to Jackie's house and while I really was hoping he would come home now, I tried to understand his want and need to be with his dad. So with tears in my eyes I hugged and kissed my baby and dropped him off with his father. When me and my kids got home, Juan was there which was a true surprise. Being at home was not his thing as of lately and I think the whole time we were in Miami me and him spoke like twice. So to know he was at home waiting on us both excited me and scared me. I wasn't sure why, but the minute my feet hit the pavement of my driveway, I got this feeling in the pit of my stomach. You know that feeling that tells you somewhere in the universe, something is about to go terribly wrong and aint shit you can do to stop it? Yep that's the one I got.

The kids were so excited to be home and they were running all around and jumping about as I stood at the front door fumbling with my door keys. I finally took a deep breath and opened it and they took off inside in search of their father. They found him immediately in the family room stretched out on the sectional watching TV. I took a deep breath and asked Jesus to be a fence and finally took a step into my home trying to convince myself that the feeling in my stomach was about nothing.

Silly me."

Keeli walks into the family room and sits down on the far end of the sectional as the kids jump all over Juan telling him about their vacation.

"We went to the beach daddy!" Ishmel informs him excitedly.
"And we went on CiCi boat." Mecca chimes in.
"Santa was there daddy. He was on the water Skis too." Asha tells him as she snuggles up to him.
"You should've came with us daddy." Ishmel tells him.
"I wish I could have, but daddy had some stuff to do here at home."
"Did Santa come here too daddy?" Asha ask sweetly.
"You know he did baby girl. And he left a whole bunch of stuff under the tree for y'all."
"Ma can we go open it?" Mecca asks excitedly.
"Please mommy?" Asha pleads.
"Go ahead." Keeli barely gets out before the kids take off across the hall into the living room where the huge 7 foot Christmas tree is. Juan and Keeli both sit there lost in the awkward silence for two full minutes until Keeli finally summons the courage to break it. "Did you take the chicken out the freezer like I asked you when I called?"
"Nah. I didn't."
"Juan……." Keeli starts to whine.
"Only because I don't want you to cook tonight. I'm gonna run the kids over to my mother house in a minute and I will stop and get us some dinner on the way back."
"And why are they going to your mother's house?"
"Because we need to talk." Juan says seriously.
"What's wrong?" Keeli asks as her eyes fill with water fearing the worse.
"Just chill Keeli. We will talk the minute I get back. As a matter of fact, I'm gonna take them over there now."
"Ok."

Juan gets up and walks out the room, leaving Keeli to sit in silence and her imagination to run wild. After getting the kids together, Juan leaves with them heading to Sissy's house. Keeli spends the next hour bringing in their luggage and unpacking. She is in Asha's room putting her things away when her personal cellphone starts ringing. It rings four times and stops signaling that voicemail has picked it up. It immediately starts ringing again. Keeli runs down the hall into the master suite and grabs her phone off the dresser and answers it.

"Hello."
"Yo Ke, come around the way NOW man! Meet me at the spot." Donna says with urgency.
"Why the fuck you calling me on this phone yo? How the fuck you even get this number?"
"I called the other joint like 10 times and you aint fucking answer! Come on man this is serious!" Donna barks.
"I know you better calm the fuck down when you speaking to me!" Keeli barks back.
"My bad yo. Just come on Ke. Shit done got real for real."
"I'm on my way." Keeli hangs up the phone before Donna can say another word.

She runs downstairs and throws on her Northface and boots and heads out to the garage and gets in her Benz. She makes a mental note that Juan's Benz is not there, although he left driving his truck. She pushes the strange things at home to the back of her mind and heads to the city. Forty minutes later she pulls up in front of Donna and Shameeka's hair salon. She walks up to the front door and knocks. Donna opens the door and she walks in and Donna's whole crew is sitting and standing around minus a few people. They all are holding looks somewhere between sad and angry.

"Alright, what the fuck is going on?" Keeli asks, feeling herself becoming annoyed already.

"We got a situation." Donna says.

"Nah this shit more than a situation yo." Devin snaps speaking out of turn.

"Yo shut the fuck up man! Aint nobody ask for your commentary and shit!" Donna snaps putting him back in his place.

"I know SOMEBODY better tell me what the fuck is going on that I was called all the way down here for this shit NOW!"

"We got hit last night." Donna says solemnly.

"Fuck you mean got hit? Got hit how?" Keeli demands to know.

"Jake B and his people came through and aired the spot out."

"You fucking kidding me right?"

"I wish. They hit the safe house."

"And what they get?" Keeli demands to know growing angrier by the second.

Donna looks over at Mikel and she lowers her head and starts to speak.. "250 cash. 8 bricks, a couple burners and....." Tears start falling out of Mikel's eyes.

"AND WHAT BITCH!" Keeli snaps, unmoved by the tears.

"Stephy, Damon, Jessee and Porche." Mo adds

"What!"

"They was on night shift." Donna says wiping her own tears. Stephy and Damon dead. Jessee in the hospital and they took Porche."

"And where the fuck was y'all at?" Keeli inquires still in shock. Nobody in the room says a word, out of fear of what would come next. "Oh so all y'all motherfuckas gone deaf now!"

"We went to the GoGo." Tara confesses.

"So y'all motherfuckas was out shaking ass while my fucking shit was being took!"

"Not all of us." Devin tries to clear things up.

"Ok so who all went. Do motherfucking tell." The room falls silent again as fear settles in and just how angry Keeli is becomes ever present. Keeli goes into her purse and pulls out her Desert Eagle and chambers a round. "So again who the fuck was at the GoGo!" Before anyone can say a word Keeli shoots Monti who is sitting closes to where she is standing in her head, sending blood and brains everywhere as she falls to the floor dead. "Now I got motherfucking bullets for days so I'm only asking one more time. Who the fuck went to the GoGo."

"Okay, okay." Tara begins to tell all. "It was me, Meeka, Donna, Shemeeka, Monti, Stephon and Korey, but we wasn't even gone that long I swear."

Keeli shoots Tara in the chest twice killing her instantly. "I hate a snitch bitch." Keeli looks around at the rest of Donna's crew who are visibly shook. "Mo, Mikel and Devin, Y'all wait for me in the parking lot." The three of them get up and exit the shop without a word. Once they leave, Keeli focuses her attention back on the remainder of the crew. "The rest of y'all motherfuckas......hold up, where the fuck is Korey and Shameeka?"

"Korey took Damon's mom to identify his body. I don't know where Shameeka at." Donna responds nervously.

"I'm holding y'all responsible for this bullshit. It's Sunday, y'all got to 11:59 Saturday to get me my fucking money. Y'all owe me 400 for them bricks, the 250 in cash and another 200 for my peoples who got hurt because of y'all shit."

"That 850,000 dollars." Stephon says in disbelief.

"I know what the fuck it is. Now like I said 11:59 or motherfuckas gonna start dying starting with y'all families." Keeli looks at Donna. "How much of my shit you got left?"

"Like 10 bricks."

"Go get my shit man."

Now?" Donna inquires dumbfounded.

"Nah tomorrow." Keeli rolls her eyes and snaps "Yes bitch NOW!" Donna heads to the back office trying to keep her emotions in check.

"So what about Porche?" Meeka inqures.

"Yo mind your fucking business and worry about coming

up with your share of my fucking money. That's the only thing should be on your mind cause I swear you will be the first bitch to catch some hot ones come Saturday if my shit aint in order." Donna comes back carrying the duffle bag and hands it to Keeli and avoids looking at her, afraid to piss her off even more. "Get this mess cleaned up and Donna, if you EVER call me on that number again, your little clan gonna have foster care sowed the fuck up cause I'mma personally see to it that they become orphans. You feel me?"
"Yeah man."

Keeli walks out the shop without another word. She puts the duffle bag in the trunk of her car then opens the door to the passenger side and sits down. She grabs a pen and paper from the glove box and writes down a number then gets out and walks over to where Mo, Mikel and Devin are waiting for her.

"So what's up boss lady? How you want us to handle this shit? You know I keep one in the chamber." Mo says eagerly and taps his gun on his hip to let Keeli know he is war ready.
"And what about Porche yo?" Devin asks with tears in her eyes.
"I know that's your family Devin, and I'm on that the moment I step off. Mo, you remember my man Ty right?"
"Yeah. The tall lightskin nigga?"
"Yeah him. This his contact. " Keeli gives Mo the paper. "Hit him up tomorrow morning. I'mma holla at him when I get in so he will be expecting your call. I'mma have you fuck with him while I get this shit straight so your pockets wont get light."
That's what's up boss lady." Mo says as he tucks the number in his back pocket.
"Devin and Mikel, I'mma get at my man Marcello and have him get up with y'all so y'all can keep eating too while this shit get sort out. I just want y'all to stay away

from them stupid motherfucka in there til shit cool. So y'all go ahead home and rest, and Devin, I'm on Porche asap so don't worry."
"Thanks Ke, my family appreciates that."
"Man chill, Porche my family too so you know I got y'all. Now I'ma get up with y'all later." Keeli hugs each of them before getting in her Benz and driving off.

"I was so fucking mad on my drive home. These bitches out in the club shaking their musty ass while niggas just running up in my shit, stealing my money, my people catching bullets and getting kidnapped like our guns don't bust. That was the first and final straw so now I had to go at this nigga Jake B. And while I wasn't scared, I was feeling some kinda way about the shit. I had never been able to put sight or sound to this nigga but his reputation preceded him to say the least. This nigga was like Freddy Kruger out this bitch. He made niggas dreams straight nightmares according to the streets, and he was proving this shit to be true by the way he was coming at my squad. But while this Jake B nigga was running around like Freddie, I slept beside a real live Michael Myers. He moved with silence and fucked up lives on the regular. So now I had to convince Juan to do what he do and make this GHOST ASS NIGGA, a real GHOST. Shit had been so tensed and crazy between me and him lately I knew I had to finesses

this shit out of him. And beside I wanted to share as little as possible with him about was really going on, so I needed a few days to work. Shit in his eyes, All I was supposed to be doing was supervising shit, not running around playing shoot em up bang bang, So I knew I was gonna have to step lightly when pulling him in.

On the way in, I called Ty and Marcello and put them down to what was going on and the people I needed them to look out for and they assured me they were on it. Since I had that out the way, I relaxed a bit and enjoyed my luxury ride home, but as I pulled into my driveway for the second time today I got a feeling in the pit of my stomach that scared the shit out of me. I got out and felt a tad bit shaky as I noticed again that Juan's Benz was not home. Juan didn't let anybody drive that bitch including me and well I married his ass. So something wasn't right. After the garage door came down, I took the gun out my purse and stuck it in the duffle bag in the trunk with the coke so I would remember to get rid of it asap. I put my game face on and walked in the house ready to do some major sucking up so I could get the ball rolling that would stop at Juan making Jake B a distance memory, but as soon as I walked in the door I stopped in my tracks. Juan was emptying the dishwasher and well the only time he did anything that resembled housework is when something was really wrong. I looked at my husband and his eyes told it all. Something was wrong. So in that instant, nothing else mattered. Not my situations with Jake B, not Porche being missing, nothing else mattered but my husband and whatever he was going through. I was the true epitome of that Sam and Dave song, When something is wrong with my baby, Something is wrong with me. Now I just had to find out WHAT was wrong."

Keeli closes the kitchen door as Juan stands up and looks at her. "Baby you didn't have to do that. I would've taken care of it." Keeli assures him.
"Nah it's cool."
"Did you get the food?"
"Yeah, it's in the oven. You was gone when I got back here."
"I'm sorry baby I had to run into the city for a second. I wasn't gone too long was I baby.?"
"Nah, you good. Look Keeli I really need to talk to you about some things."
"Ok, I'll make our plates and we can sit down and talk over dinner."
Juan observes all the potential weapons in the kitchen.
"Nah, lets go talk in the family room. It won't take long I promise."
"Ok I guess. I hope I don't die of starvation." Keeli jokes as she heads down the hall to the family room with Juan on her heels. They walk in and Keeli sits down on the sectional and Juan sits on the ottoman. Juan takes a deep

breath and starts talking before he loses his nerve.

"Keeli, I know you gonna flip, but I would rather you hear it from me."

"Oh.My. God! You having an affair aren't you!

"No! I mean not exactly."

"So what are you telling me Juan? What the fuck are you saying to me!!"

"Just calm down Keeli please!"

"Calm down! What the fuck do you mean calm down! You tell me you fucking around on me and I'm supposed to be fucking calm!" Keeli jumps up and runs for the exit as the tears start to fall from her eyes. Juan tries to grab her and she starts swinging wildly. He lets go and she runs out into the hallway and sits on the stairs and lets the tears of hurt and betrayal fall uninterrupted. Juan comes out into the hallway and sits on the floor in front of her.

"I'm sorry Keeli. You know the last thing I would ever want to do is hurt you baby."

"You have a funny way of not hurting me buddy." Keeli chuckles still in disbelief.

"It wasn't like that Ke."

"That's soooooo fucking typical. So what happened Juan? You just tripped, fell and landed in this bitch pussy!! Do tell!"

"Look Keeli, I'm a man and I can admit my faults and when I fucked up. I never meant to hurt you but I fucked up big this time Keeli!"

Keeli looks up at Juan with her tear drenched face and notices his eyes are holding tears of their own. "So what are you looking for Juan? Forgiveness?

"Baby I don't know what I'm looking for. I'm so confused right now." The tears that Juan have been trying to hide start to silently slip down his face, breaking Keeli's heart even more.

"Do you...... do you love her Juan?" Keeli forces herself to ask the painful question she is certain she already knows the answer to."

Juan looks down at the floor, his guilt preventing him from looking into his wife's eyes. "Not as much as I love you Keeli."

"That's the biggest croc of bullshit I've ever fucking heard!!"

"It's not bullshit Keeli! I'm trying to be fucking honest with you!"

"Who is it Juan! Is it that bitch Niema?"

"Hell no!

"So what it's some random ho you done fucking met out in these streets and now you think you love the bitch!"

"No!"

"So who the fuck is she Juan! Who is the bitch!"

"It's Randi Keeli!" The words fly out of Juan's mouth and sucks the wind out of the entire house. He stands up and looks at Keeli not knowing what to expect next.

"Ever since the day I met Juan back in Georgetown all those years ago, I never felt anything in my heart for this man other than love. Even when we were apart, as mad as I was living without him, my heart never felt anything other than love for him. I thought I didn't know HOW to feel anything different for him..... that was, until this very moment.

The words he spoke, they hurt way more than the night that bullet tore through my leg. That shit was a cakewalk compared to this. It was like my body took a few seconds to fully process what Juan had just said to me and from there, I became a stark raving fucking lunatic. I flew off the stairs and was in full attack mode. I don't know what the

fuck I was yelling at him, but know I was yelling it with every ounce of me as I threw punches with all the fuck I had inside. I hated the man before me and I wanted to take his life with my bare fucking hands. And he knew he was fucked up wrong because in any other situation Juan would have swole the fuck up and shut me down, this night, all my husband could do was try and pin me to the floor but forgive my French, my ass was retarded strong that night. I was out for blood. The same pain in my heart I wanted him to feel, shit I wanted it to be worse.

At some point, Juan got me pinned down on the floor and I looked up into those green eyes that used to be able to kiss away all the pain in this world. Those same eyes I trusted with my. life. Those eyes that stood before the entire fucking world and said I was the only one for him..... I felt nothing but hate when I looked into those eyes. This was truly the beginning of the end. I was beyond done with this shit."

Keeli stops fighting and looks up at Juan. "Let me go please." She says calmly.
"No. Not until you calm down."
"Juan, I'm as calm as I'ma get so please just get off of me."
"Can we just talk about this Keeli? Please baby."

"I listened to all that I'm gonna listen to that has come out of your mouth Juan, now it's my turn to talk."
"Just talk right? No more fighting?" Juan asks in hopes of clarification.
"No more fighting. I promise." Keeli says with a smile.
"Ok." Juan lets go of Keeli and stands up. Keeli gets up off the floor and wipes her eyes then readjusts her shirt. She wipes away the strands of her hair that managed to cover her face during the fight. She looks at Juan and smiles again.
"Get out." Keeli says calmly.
"What?" Juan asks hoping he heard her wrong.
"Oh you heard me." Keeli's smile fades immediately. "Get your shit and get the fuck out!"
"Keeli listen, can we just talk about this please?" Juan pleads.
"Oh no honey. Me and your trifling ass are so DONE talking. Now by the time I get back, you NEED to have gathered all your shit and got the fuck up outta my space or I'm telling you Juan, Sissy not gonna like me cause I promise she will be burying your ass." Keeli steps closer to Juan and looks him in his eyes showing not an ounce of fear. "Now fucking try me." Juan stands there completely speechless looking at Keeli, unsure of what to say or do at this point. "Now I'ma let your sorry ass pack in peace." Keeli turns and walks out of the family room leaving Juan standing in the middle of the floor completely speechless. She walks down the hall into the kitchen and walks out the side door. She opens the trunk of her Benz and takes the dirty gun out of the duffle bag. Juan opens the door and freezes when Keeli turns around with the gun in her hand.
"Keeli listen, it's no need for that. Can we please just talk about all of this."
"Any talking you care to do can be done in the presence of my attorney. Now like I said Juan, please get your shit and get the fuck up out my house by time I get back." Keeli chambers a round and looks at him. "Cause I swear

I wont stop pulling this motherfucka until it's empty and you full." Keeli walks over to the wall and hits the button causing the garage door to open. She walks out and down the driveway and gets in her Range Rover and drives off, leaving Juan standing there speechless.

"I wanted to cry so bad, but I was too fucking angry to form tears. In a way, as silly as it may sound I blamed myself. I should have seen this shit coming. I saw through Randi stanking ass from day one. So why the fuck didn't I just murder her snake in the grass ass and keep it moving? I was too busy playing fucking Sally Homemaker while all three of these motherfuckas lied right in my face. This bitch was fucking MY HUSBAND right under my fucking nose the whole time. They caught me slipping and I felt so stupid. At this point, all the hurt I was feeling, I felt I deserved for not keeping my eyes wide open.

I rode around aimlessly for a while debating my next move. I didn't want to be alone but a part of me was too embarrassed to reach out to anybody for comfort. I was the fucking Queen out here in these streets. I was far from the kinda bitch one would cheat on, so I didn't understand it. My pride was hurt and my ego was bruised as a motherfucka. It was bitches out in this world that went to bed every night wishing they was me, so what the fuck made him think it was OK for him to go and hang dick up in this basic bitch? I thought about going to a bar and literally drowning myself in alcohol. I wanted to be numb so my heart wouldn't hurt anymore. But while my heart said bar, my mind said nope and before I even realized it, I was pulling up in Sissy's driveway. I thought at first my mind lead me here to pick up my kids so I could have them by my side to keep me from going on a murder spree, BUT when I saw Juan's Benz sitting in the driveway of Sissy's house, my women's intuition let me know I was there for a whole different reason."

Keeli parks her truck behind Juan's Benz and gets out. She walks up to the house and rings the doorbell then stands and waits patiently. A minute later, Sam opens the door and Keeli walks in smiling.

"What's up fathead." Keeli jokes.
"Hey Ke. I thought Juan was coming to pick the kids up in the morning." Sam questions, feeling uneasy about Keeli's pop up.
"Nah, change of plans." Keeli responds as they make their way down the hall and into the Great Room where Sissy, Shane, Randi and Markee are sitting and talking. Keeli chuckles at the sight before her.
"Hey Boo." Shane greets Keeli and stands up. Keeli walks over and hugs her.
"Hey Love." Keeli says then turns to look at Sissy. "Sissy where my kids at?"
"Well hello to you too." Sissy rolls her eyes.

"They downstairs with Fredricko. He putting together that pool table thing Ma got them."

"Cool." Keeli turns and looks at Randi. "Maranda, can I speak to you right quick?"

"Oh,oh Ok." Randi studders. "What's up?"

"Nah it's a private matter. Let's walk outside."

"Wait a minute." Sissy interrupts. "How was Miami Keeli."

"Same way it always is." Keeli responds curtly then refocuses her attention on Randi. "Maranda..."

"Okay, here I come." Randi stands up nervously as Keeli walks out the Great Room and walks back down the hall and out the front door.

"Now what the hell she want with you?" Sissy inquires.

"I don't know Ma." Randi says nervously.

"I pray this dumb ass boy aint went and told her." Sissy shakes her head.

"Well maybe we should hang close by the front door just in case." Markee adds.

"She cool. If Keeli knew what was going on, she would've came through the door swinging and y'all know it. Just go head on Randi before she start tripping." Shane adds.

Randi puts on her jacket and leave out the room. She walks outside and over to Keeli who is leaning against Juan's Benz smoking a cigarette.

"Damn, I aint know it was this cold out here." Randi tries to break the tension filled ice.

"Fuck all that. Is there something you wanna tell me Maranda?"

"No. Nothing I can think of offhand."

"You sure?" Keeli asks growing more irritated.

"I'm positive." Randi assures her.

Keeli drops the cigarette on the ground and closes the distance between the two of them. "So you don't want to tell me that you've been fucking my husband?" Keeli asks calmly. Randi drops her head in shame and looks away.

"So I take that as a yes." Keeli asks sarcastically.
"Keeli…. " Maranda starts to explain. "When I first came here, trust me it was not my intentions to get back together with Juan. But we both realized that those old feelings we thought were gone were still there. Please don't think we were purposely trying to hurt you because we weren't. It just happened."
"It just happened huh." Keeli chuckles at the statement.
"Yes." Randi responds and an awkward silence settles between the two women. "I really need to go back inside because…."

Keeli hauls off and punches Randi in her face knocking her to the ground. She starts kicking and stomping Randi in the face, chest and stomach while ranting and raving about killing the bitch. Randi is screaming at the top of her lungs for help while trying desperately to protect herself from Keeli's assault to no avail. Sissy, Markee and Shane come running out of the house as Randi tries to crawl away from Keeli who is yanking her by her hair and kicking her repeatedly. Shane and Markee grab Keeli and are finally able to pry her hands out of Randi's hair and pull her away. Sissy helps Randi up off the ground and Randi takes off running and goes in the house.

"What the fuck is wrong with you girl!" Sissy screams at Keeli in her thick Jamaican accent.
"Aint shit wrong with me! Tell that bitch to come the fuck back outside!"
"Get off my property Keeli! This is not Northeast. Take that ghetto shit back over there!"
"Fuck you Sissy!"
"Fuck you too! I wish every day Juan had left your ratchet ass in the slums where he found you at."
"Just get my fucking kids!"
"Just get in the car Keeli, I will get them." Markee shouts while trying to help Shane get Keeli back to her truck.
"Ok, just get them so I can go." Keeli says calmly. Markee

runs back across the lawn and goes into the house.
"Come on Keeli, please lets just go. This bitch is not worth all this." Shane tries to reason with Keeli. Keeli looks at Shane with tears rolling down her face. "This bitch is fucking my husband Shane! My fucking husband!" Keeli yells as the tears and hurt began pouring out of her.
"I know you hurt Keeli, but just come on and let me take you home. Or just come to my house so you can get away from all this madness."
"I'm not going NO FUCKING WHERE until I get my kids."
"You are way too upset to take them any Goddamn where!" Sissy yells from her position on the lawn.
"Fuck you bitch! I know your old stanking miserable ass had a fucking hand in this. Your phony ass been hating me since day one cause I'm everything your nothing ass aint. Bitch Ian MADE YOU, I'm self made and aint need your fucking son for NOTHING I have! You wanted our marriage to fail just like yours you simple bitch!!"
"Shane, get this trashy bitch off my property! This is the last time I'ma say it. Next I'm calling the police!"
"Call the police bitch! Fuck you and them! I'll whoop your ass and that bitch ass in front of the police!"
"Suit yourself bitch." Sissy goes back in her house and slams the door.
Shane pushes Keeli towards her truck again. "Keeli what the fuck is wrong with you! That's Juan's MOTHER you just threatened. Your kids GRANDMOTHER."
"What's wrong with ME? This tramp is fucking my husband and this old miserable bitch more than likely set it up and you got the nerve to ask what the fuck is wrong with ME! Who the fuck side are you on for real Shane cause you sound like you team THEM right the fuck now!"
"Keeli shut the fuck up cause you tripping! Bitch you my family and I'm tryna save your stupid ass! You just fucking ASSULTED a PREGNANT WOMAN in fucking POTOMAC MARYLAND.... Bitch what the fuck you think about to go down now!"
Keeli stands there speechless with her mouth hanging

open feeling as though her heart has been completely torn out of her chest. "Pregnant?"

"Keeli listen….. " Shane tries to back pedal kicking herself for letting that detail slip.

"Pregnant?" Keeli asks again in a tone that is barely audible. "THIS BITCH IS FUCKING PREGNANT!!" Keeli shoves Shane out of her way and Shane falls to the ground as Keeli takes off running at full speed to the house. She runs into the house and Randi is in the Great Room on the phone with the police. Keeli punches her in the face knocking her into the glass curio stand causing it to fall and break. Keeli starts to relentlessly stomp and kick Randi again. Markee, Sissy and Fredricko run out of the basement when they hear the commotion. When they get into the Great Room Keeli is on top of Randi with a tight grip on her hair repeatedly banging her face into the floor. Fredricko and Markee grab Keeli and try to pry her off but she will not let go.

All the kids come running upstairs and Sissy yells and orders them back downstairs while trying to hold off Infiniti who is trying to get to her mother's rescue and calling Keeli all kinds of bitches and screaming that she hates her. Fredricko picks Keeli up by her waist and yanks her while Markee has Randi by her arms and is trying to pull her in the opposite direction. When Fredricko yanks Keeli, she pulls out a huge hunk of Randi's hair from the roots and they are finally separated. Just then Juan and Shane run into the house. They are met in the hallway by Fredricko who has Keeli thrown across his shoulder and she is kicking and screaming about killing Randi.

"What the fuck is going on!" Juan demands to know.
"Man I don't know!" Fredricko replies honestly.
"It was that bitch!" Sissy yells while storming behind them placing all the blame on Keeli. "She brought her stupid ghetto ass over here and jumped on that girl for

nothing and cussed me out! The bitch is crazy Juan and I'm glad you finally leaving that bitch!"

"Shut the fuck up Ma!" Juan yells as he runs outside behind Fredricko. Fredricko takes Keeli down to the lawn and lays her down on the grass.

"Keeli listen….." Juan attempts to reason with her again.

"Fuck you bitch!" Keeli yells as she jumps up off the ground and charges at Juan. He grabs her by her waist and picks her up in the air and slams her down hard on the hood of his Benz. He climbs on top of her and holds her down by her arms.

"Keeli I swear I don't want to fucking hurt you. Just get the kids and go the fuck home!"

"Fuck you nigga! I aint going nowhere until I kill that bitch and your messy ass mother and your sorry ass too!" Keeli spits at Juan's face and he moves just in the nick of time to avoid it. He draws back and is about to punch her in the face when 6 Montgomery County police cars pull up on Sissy's property and 12 officers jump out with their guns drawn. Juan climbs off of Keeli with his hand up.

"I knew I had royally fucked up then. They sent 12 of the redneckest motherfuckas Mo County had on the force out there to see what was going down with the niggas in the neighborhood. They were ready to haul Me, Juan, Fredricko, and Shane to jail because we were all in the driveway where the fight was going on and they couldn't make sense of what was what at first. In the end, they only ended up cuffing me and taking me away.

Pissed was too calm a word to describe what

I was feeling. After they cuffed me, read me my rights and put me in the back of the squad car, I had the pleasure of sitting there and watching the ambulance come and take Randi ass off to the hospital. Infiniti rode in the ambulance with her and seeing that hurt. Although she was Randi's biological daughter, I had spent so many years as her mother. I loved her little ass like she was mine. So it hurt to see her throw me to the side and roll with the bitch who left her behind. One thing I was glad about though, was that Juan wasn't stupid enough to call himself getting in the ambulance and riding to the hospital with that bitch cause God knows them officers would have more than likely had to shoot my ass cause not even them handcuffs and the one sided doors of a police car would have stopped me from getting to their asses then.

Since it was long after 5pm, I didn't get to see a judge. I had to go before the commissioner and that stanking ass white bitch pissed me clean the fuck off, so I TOLD her to go fuck herself and she gave me some time to cool off. No bail, and sent my ass on to the slammer.

I had to wait 3 ½ hours to be processed and then another two hours for shift change, and count before I was put in population. Once I got to my cell, I just sat there. I didn't cry or anything. I just sat there completely pissed thee fuck off.

Pissed with myself.

Here I was, a motherfucking BILLIONAIRE. The QUEEN OF DC. I had been moving MAJOR weight throughout the United States for more than a decade at this point. I had a total of 13 bodies under my belt and had NEVER got so much as a fucking speeding ticket. Now here I am, a certified FED NIGGA, sitting in jail on a fucking ASSULT AND DISTURBING THE PEACE CHARGES.

What type of pure bullshit was this!

I had broke my number one rule and that shit had me so disgusted with myself I couldn't even think about the people who cause this shit anymore. All I could think about was the fact that my number one rule had been NEVER REACT OFF EMOTIONS. Because when you do, you either end up dead or in jail. And now look at me. Fucking crown sitting at the property desk.

I was so fucked up I didn't even bother to call nobody.

The next day I was back in court and I guess

the Commissioner had spoke with the judge about my disrespectful ass because I got sent right back over the jail. Tia, was there to represent me and she barely got a word in because the judge pretty much said fuck me and stepped my ass right back. Juan was there and I couldn't understand why. I had no rap for this nigga and wanted nothing to do with him. If his sorry ass had kept his dick in his pants, I wouldn't even have been in there anyway so my tone was fuck him and it was ringing loud and clear.

The next day, Tia came to see me on a lawyer visit. She let me know these petty motherfuckas had stepped my charges up to attempted murder. Randi had a miscarriage and had to get 45 stitches in her face and they were talking about she would need hair transplants because I had snatched her shit out by the roots. So she was sporting the George Jefferson up top. And my little disturbing the peace charge had been upgrading to breaking and entering. That was all Sissy doing and according to Tia, this bitch was determined to push forward with the charges even though Juan was begging her not to. She was even mad with Tia for representing me. The mention of him caused me to get angry all over again. All this shit was his fault, so I didn't need his ass outside wearing Free Keeli shirts. All I needed him to do was keep his dick in his pants and represent team US. But he let me down so I aint need or want his ass on my side of the court anymore. I told Tia it was, what it was in regards to her mother, but tell her brother his support or help is not needed so stay the fuck away from me, even in the courtroom.

When Tia left me, I finally cried. Those new charges and the fact that my mother-in-law was prepared to send me to jail got to me. But I also knew Tia was a damn good attorney and she was on her J.O.B at all times. I mean shit, if she could get Monae ass a walk on a DOUBLE murder beef I KNEW she could get me a skate for beating a bitch ass.

Three days later, I went back up for a bail review and this time the judge set my shit at 250,000 dollars and I was being fined 5,000 dollars for my remark to the Commissioner. The next morning Juan got a bond for 25,000 and I was sprung. I claimed my property and he was waiting to pick me up. I didn't want to get in no damn car with him but I needed to get home. So I sucked it up and let him give me a ride home.

The hour long ride from Jessup to our house seemed extra long. Like traffic and shit was just everywhere for no reason causing me to have to breathe the same air as his sorry ass *for way longer than I could stand. I aint say a mumbling word to his ass and when he pulled up in the driveway of MY house, I hopped out his Range Rover and slammed his door so hard I'm surprised that bitch aint fall to the ground. I went in the house and slammed and locked my door without looking back and got straight on the phone with a locksmith and ADT. I needed my locks changed and the security codes cause he no longer lived here and didn't need to have access to my home.*

Juan came back and hour later with the kids and dropped them off. They had been at Roc's house, where he was now staying because apparently, shit was not cool between him and his stupid ass mother at this point. He stood in the driveway looking pathetic as shit as the kids came in the house. Once they were in I closed the door and he left. I guess he called himself respecting the fact that I aint have no words for him. I decided that night that even though I was done with his ass I was gonna hold off on the divorce filings until AFTER my criminal case went to trial. Talking to Tia, she advised me to wait because it would look better for me. I was a hurt wife who lost it which was true. I also decided to hold off on dealing with Jake B because well, I wasn't asking Juan to do JACK SHIT for me right now. So I needed time to figure out how to handle this nigga on my own.

Since I now had an open criminal case on the books, I had to make sure my hands STAYED clean so I switched up my game plan again. Since I was HOT, I wasn't about to leave the country to travel to Columbia personally, so I put the only nigga I felt could handle the responsibility of being the BOSS in charge. My ACE in the hole.

Ty.

Me and Ian arranged a new plan for my shipment. Now it was gonna be flown from Columbia to Mexico, then driven into the United States via the Arizona border. That's where Ty was to check in at because even though I loved Ty and trusted him with my life and my business, My father in law aint want the nigga standing on the same continent as him. Ian didn't do new friends at all so this is how we had to roll. Once Ty checked the shit in and handed over the money, the weight would be driven back to DC in Uhaul trucks because they didn't have to stop at the weigh stations. This was partially Juan's old set up when he was touching the dope. And since Ian had some Border Patrol officers in pocket, coming across the border would never be a problem. All the coke would be packed in furniture so in the event they got stopped once on the road to DC, it looked like it was just a cross country move or something.

Since I didn't have to make them trips down to Columbia anymore, I sold my private plane and invested that money in a small "U Store it" storage company our in Riverdale Maryland and it was gonna be used to store the work once it came in.

I also realized I really couldn't afford to have a bunch of enemies on the streets right now and was smart enough to know that, I worked out a deal with Donna and her crew of fuck ups. I put them on a payment plan as far as my money but they was cut off from QDC until I got that 850 from them. I guess that was better than being dead.

About a month after all that shit went down, Porche finally turned up. Unfortunately she was DEAD. Her body was found way out in Springfield Virginia. She had been raped, starved and finally beaten to death. I felt so bad but I kinda already knew she was dead. Nobody is gonna hold you hostage for about 30 days and then just say fuck it go home. When they snatched her and no word came in about a ransom, I knew she was already dead or they planned to kill her the moment they grabbed her. I got with Devin and gave her and her family some money to help pay for the services. That was about all I could do at that point.

In April, we had a status hearing on my case, and even though Sissy had FINALLY dropped the charges against me, I guess because her son completely stopped speaking to her ass.... Randi and the State of Maryland was still pushing forward. They set a trial date that was damn near a year off. March 8th, 2005. My 30th birthday. Since I had a serious amount of time to kill, I threw myself into my work and my family. Then I got the break that I needed. The shit just fell right into my lap."

"BACKTIGHT"

May 2004

"Over the past few months, I had managed to build a civil relationship with Juan. We agreed to split custody of the kids 50/50. He took them every other week since he had moved into one of his investment properties out in Bethesda. I still hadn't filed for my divorce yet because aside from the whole criminal trial shit, a part of me still loved and wanted Juan. It was crazy because just like before, I didn't want to love him anymore. I wanted my heart to be free because that shit with Maranda was a true blow to my heart. But the thing about love is, it aint like a faucet that you can just turn on and off at your own free will. Love, real love was something that bloomed way down deep within your heart, mind and spirit and you have absolutely no control over it. So it wasn't my choice to keep loving Juan. But our history together wouldn't allow me not to. I wouldn't admit it to anybody but I was lonely as hell without him. Sleeping in that big ass custom made king size bed was pure torture not being able to roll over and stick my head up under his armpit in the middle of the night. Or have him roll over at 3am and rub that thang up against my ass until I started to stir then ask "babe, you sleep?" I missed him so much. I can't even fake with you but I held my head. As bad as I wanted

to I couldn't just let him come home and take him back like that. He had to feel what life was really like without me first. I felt that was the only way he would see the value in what we shared again.

Me and Jackie were building this amazing co-parenting/ friendship thing surrounding CiCi. And while I will admit, when he first came on the scene I wasn't feeling no parts of his shit, but at this point, I was glad to have him around. We talked like every day about our son and just life in general. He had met a chick and they were rocking tough. She was cute, but she was no me. But she was good for Jackie. When they moved in together, I had to meet her because my son was living there and I needed to make sure she knew where the boundary line was. Her name was Tarissa, and it was funny seeing Jackie hold the same gleam in his eye when he spoke about her that he used to hold for me. Me and him had a conversation one day where we both realized we had reached the same point in life. The point where you know what it's like to truly love someone but NOT be in love with them. I loved Jackie. He was my first love, my first everything and the father of my first born. And to have him back in our lives, being a stand up dude teaching his son how to be a man, I not only loved him but I appreciated him. But I was no longer IN LOVE with him which is why I was able to accept Tarissa as long as she treated BOTH OF THEM right. Because truth be told, Jackie was a good dude. He said he felt the same thing about me. He loved me for loving him as strong as I did. For giving him his first and only and for being the rock I was when he was away and making all the sacrifices I did for our son. But likewise, he was no longer in love with me. He admitted when he first came home, he lived with this notion that we would get back together, fall madly in love with each other again and get married. Then he said the first time he saw me with Juan, he knew I was not only happy but IN LOVE and I deserved that. So it took a while but eventually he got over me.

Although me and Jackie were building a beautiful friendship, there was an elephant in the room that we had never talked about.

Me and Simm.

He asked me once and the guilt of stabbing him in the back with his best friend was unbearable and all I could do was cry. I couldn't form the words to get anything out. I just cried because even back then, I knew that shit was hella wrong. Even though Jackie was away, it was wrong. And in hindsight, the reason I started parting my legs for this nigga was trife. But at that time *in life it was all about survival and that's what I was trying to do. Survive. Jackie, being the stand up dude he had become just held me and told me it was ok. I guess seeing my guilt let him know I didn't set out on a mission to hurt him. After that one time, he never brought up the Keeli and Simm drama again. And I appreciated that more than words could express.*

While the relationships in my life were moving into different places, so was my legal and legit endeavors. I was writing the final chapter of my book and working with the cover designers because I needed that thing to POP. Me and Ciaira had also set the opening date for our Boutique "K and C's House of Fab." It was set for the last Saturday in June and was gonna be a big Ta-DO. Ciaira had been pulling out her big boy cards and talking to some majors in the fashion industry and was able to get us and our lines invited to an exclusive fashion show in Milan. This thing was for big names and big wigs, BUT when your money was longer than a football field, two unknown chicks from fucking E Street were able to hop a private plane and eat caviar and rub elbows with motherfuckas with names we could barely pronounce.

Yep despite all the dumb shit, we were LIVING beyond our wildest dreams.

Since fashion was truly Ciaira thing, her passion and I was really just in this to well clean up some money, she took front and center on the whole thing and made our arrangements for Milan. Only thing was, we were gonna have to be there for a whole month. Ciaira was gonna send her kids down south with her mother during that time. I thought about leaving my kids with Dana BUT Dana had her a man and wasn't really checking for months with Grandma no more. So I had to convince Juan to play Mr. Mom for a whole month to our offspring. I could have just asked, but I told him we were done and now here I was asking for favors and shit. I stayed in deep thought for a couple of days and also prayed on it and finally picked up the phone and called Juan out of the blue and invited him to dinner. He was shocked, but he accepted the invitation so I knew we were off to a good start.

I made reservations at Fogo de Chao and was damn lucky to get a table for that night. I dropped the kids off with Dana then went shopping, got a pedi and a mani then went home. Syrus and Lamai came over and hung out with me for a while and then I went and got myself together for my dinner date with my estranged husband.

I was trying to accomplish two things that

night. Get him to agree to keep the kids and let him see what he was truly missing. I wanted my husband back and when I prayed on it, I felt ok about trying to work through this with him. So my goal for this night was to get my husband back 100%. I covered my skin that night.... And not too much of it with a black Alexander McQueen leather ruffle dress. My ass made that thing look amazing. I paired my dress with my Alexander McQueen ankle tie snake embossed leather sandals. The 4 and a half inch heel had me feeling some kinda sexy. I was praying Juan took one look at me and realized what he left behind with his affair and begged to get his shit right. Our reservations were for 9, so I jumped in my Benz and headed for the city.

When I got there, Juan was standing outside, flowers in hand waiting on my arrival. He was rocking black Gucci from head to toe and he looked damn good. My pussy started thumping the minute I laid eyes on him. Shit, it had only been 4 months since Papi left me breathless with my legs shaking. I instantly started regretting my decision NOT to wear panties that evening. Last thing I wanted to do was be leaking all over these people chairs.

I got out my ride and handed my keys to the valet and when Juan smiled at me, I just wanted my husband back. I walked up to him and we exchanged a hug and he kissed me on my cheek and it left me with goose pimples all over my body. I not only wanted this man, I NEEDED him. Juan was my everything. I just prayed that 4 months apart had showed him that I was his everything also."

Juan subconsciously licks his lips as he hold Keeli at arm's length and stares at her smiling, taking in all her beauty. "You look beautiful tonight Keeli."

"Thank you." Keeli blushes. "You don't look too bad yourself. Have you been waiting long?"

"Nah. About 10, 15 minutes. I was just standing out here thinking about our first date. When you had me standing outside waiting for you then too with your slow moving ass." Juan chuckles.

Keeli blushes at the memory. "Friday's in Gtown. One of the best dates I ever had."

"Well even though you asked me out this time, let's see if I can top that one this evening."

"You can try." Keeli teases as she blows Juan an air kiss.

"I most certainly will. Come on, let's get inside. Oh wait, these are for you." Juan hands Keeli the expensive flower bouquet. She accepts it and smiles at him.

"You one uping Juan from 1995 already. Me likes, me likes."

Juan laughs as he holds Keeli's free hand and they enter the restaurant together. After they are seated at their table, Juan orders a bottle of wine for the two of them. He looks at Keeli and smiles as soon as the waiter goes to get the wine. "So what do I owe the honor of having dinner with the most beautiful woman in the world this evening?"

"Nothing really. I like food, you like food." Keeli teases.

"Yeah." Juan laughs. "And we both have food at our houses so what's truly the deal?"

"Alright. Truth is..." Keeli sighs. "I've been missing you."

"Say what now?" Juan smiles.

"Yes. It gets pretty lonely sleeping in that big ass bed alone. I think that's why you had that thing built so if we ever ended up here, I would miss your ass." Keeli and Juan both laugh.

"Perhaps. But seriously, I know the feeling. That's why I don't even sleep in my bed. I be crashing on the couch."

"Well you know how I feel about bodies on my sofas."

"Yeah yeah yeah I know. How could I not. How many times have you bit my head off for falling asleep on the one in the living room." Juan smiles at the memory. "I miss that."

Keeli blushes. "I miss you."

"Keeli, I miss you more than I can even put the words together to express and that's no lie. I messed up bad Keeli but if you......."

"Juan slow down." Keeli reaches across the table and grabs his hands and begins to caress them. "We will get to that. But right now, let's just enjoy this time together."

"You right." Juan smiles. "Hey, you wanna dance?"

"I would love to." Juan stand up and walks over to Keeli. When she stands up, he grabs her hand and they walk over to where the live band is playing and begin to slow dance.

"The funny thing was, there was no dance floor so to speak. Me and Juan were in our own world. We held on to each other for dear life and just got lost in each other and

the music. It reminded me of our first dance at our wedding reception. I can't speak for Juan, but I forgot about the packed house around us that day. All I knew was Juan and I like to think all he knew was me. I opened my eyes at one point and you could see couples and people at their tables just smiling at us. I guess our love was felt all over the restaurant. We danced together for about 10 minutes and then the manager showed up. He explained that they didn't really allow dancing, although he felt the love we were sharing, so we went back to our table.

We shared some laughs, ate good, drank until the bottle was just about empty and just enjoyed each other's company. The manager brought us dessert because we were so cute and according to him, you don't see lots of people truly in love these days. Me and Juan both thanked him and accepted the death by chocolate cake. We both had a bite or two and then I invited Juan back to my house for dessert. I was barely finished talking and his ass was signaling the waiter for the check. Since he was a gentlemen, he paid for dinner and we both headed to the valet. I got in my Benz and he got in his Rover and we headed for Potomac. We both had the same thing on our minds, but I wasn't giving it up that easy. Although I wanted to fuck Juan just as bad as I wanted

to breathe my next breath, if not more, he had to work for this pussy at this point. I mean hey, it was HIS FAULT he hadn't been getting it. So yeah, his ass needed to put in work if he wanted to feel these walls."

Keeli uses her keys to open the door and Juan follows her inside. She goes straight to the alarm and disables it. When she turns around, Juan is standing right behind her with sexual hunger in his eyes. He grabs Keeli and pulls her to him and kisses her softly. Keeli nibbles on his bottom lip and they begin to taste each other's tongues. Keeli throws her arms around Juan's neck and he unzips the back of her dress and begins to try and take it off of her while they are still engaged in their kiss. Keeli pulls away and steps back from Juan. Juan looks at her confused with a bulge in the front of his pants that he makes no attempt to hide. "What's wrong baby?" He inquires, not understanding why Keeli pulled away. "What are you doing?" Keeli asks in a serious tone. "What I'm doing? You invited me over for dessert." Juan moves closer to Keeli and grabs her waist and pulls her back to him and kisses her lips softly. "I was helping myself to some dessert." "Okay, this is awkward." Keeli chuckles in a nervous tone and steps back from Juan. "When I said dessert, I was talking about the strawberry cheesecake I made. I know how you feel about strawberry chessecake and thought you might like a slice or two." "Are you serious Keeli?" Juan ask in disbelief. "Yes I'm serious. Oh you thought....... Well I hate to be the one to tell you, but I got my visitor. Look, just go wait in the family room and I will bring you a slice." Keeli turns and goes down the hall into the kitchen and Juan goes in the family room trying to hide his pisstivity. He sits down on the sofa and starts to thumb through a magazine. Not actually looking at it, just trying to take his focus off the brick hard dick in his pants.

About 5 minutes later, just as he gets his hormones under control, Keeli yells down the hall and summons Juan to the kitchen. He puts the magazine down and lets out an irritated sigh not wanting no damn cheesecake….. just some pussy. He walks down the hall trying to check his attitude because he didn't want to ruin the chance at reconciliation. He walks into the kitchen and stops in his tracks and smiles as his dick instantly gets 4 times harder than it was before.

Keeli is completely naked, with chocolate lines on her thighs, tracing over her abdomen and up to her breast. She has a chocolate circle going around each one and her nipples are covered in chocolate. She is laying on the kitchen counter in a Betty Boop type pose with a strawberry in her mouth. She takes the strawberry out her mouth, spreads her legs and rubs the strawberry against her softest place then holds it out for Juan. "You want a bite?" She asks in her most seductive voice. With a smile on his face spread a mile long, Juan closes the distance between them.

"As I always said, what's understood needs no discussion and um, Juan understood me very well. After he devoured the Keeli flavored strawberry, I threw my head back in pure ecstasy as his tongue traced every line of chocolate on my body. When he got to my breast and took the first nipple into his mouth, I felt a puddle form under me instantly. My body was on FIRE at this

point. By the time he released the second nipple and had them swollen as hell, looking like two big ass thumbs, I was begging him to taste this pussy. Juan tongue game was NO JOKE and I needed that shit in my life. And like the perfect husband, he obliged. He at that pussy until I was LITERALLY crying and begging him to stop. I came 3 times and he just kept going. I was too weak fucking with him.

He finally came up and I was ready to put my head game down but he told me he NEEDED to be inside of me NOW and he couldn't wait any longer. I pulled him to me and we started to kiss as he lift me up and carried me over to the kitchen table. He placed me down on it, never breaking our kiss and I worked on his buttons, popping most of them as he freed the one eyes monster from its cage. Juan placed his dick against my opening and begin to enter me. He had to grip the edged of the table to contain himself because my shit was so tight and so wet. While he gripped the table, I gripped him because that mix of pleasure and pain was too much. Juan took his time with me, as he always did and worked that big motherfucka all the way in. And once he was in there.....HE WAS IN THERE.

It took about 5 minutes of his stroke game and my snap game and we both were *holding on to each other taking that ride into pure sexual bliss together. We both came so hard it was UGLY. Juan held me close until every single drop of him was inside of me. When he pulled out, I slid off the table and dropped down to my knees and begin to take him into my mouth. I can't lie, I had been wanting to suck Juan's dick since I stepped out my car at the restaurant that night. I laid my head game down until his dick was standing back at full attention. When he was hard as a brick again, I lead him over to the highback barstools and had him sit down. I straddled him and rode that dick like a champ. Between the biting, the ass smacking, and tiddie sucking I was in HEAVEN. We went from the barstool to the floor, doggy style, to the shower with me pinned against the wall taking it like a champ and finally to the bed. It was 90 minutes of the greatest make up sex ever. We ended things with me on my knees sucking the soul out his dick until he couldn't take it anymore and sent the whole package flying down the back of my throat.*

We laid there, sweaty and wrapped in each other's arm breathing heavy and tingly all over. Next thing I knew, the sun was creeping through my bedroom windows.

We spent the entire day shopping and having quality time. I missed my husband so much and could tell from the way he was constantly loving up on me, grabbing me up for unexpected kisses and just smiling and enjoy the sound of my voice that he missed me too and had more than likely been on his knees every night during our separation just like me asking GOD to give us another try.

I smiled as I thought about something my Grandma Vickey used to say back in the day as far as men. If you love a man and he hand you ass to kiss up close, hand him yours from afar and watch how shit change. I was positive that Juan got it and we wouldn't be walking down that road of hurt and confusion again for the rest of our lives.

And for that, I was thankful."

"Maranda's Secrete"

"Juan wasted absolutely NO TIME bringing his ass home. The next day his shit was home and back in drawers before the sun set. The kids were beyond excited to have both of us together in the same house again.

I gave him about 3 full days of being home before I sprung my month long business trip to Milan on him. He was cool with it since it was business. But considering what we had just went through I think if it wasn't business related he would of still been cool with shit out of fear that I might put my skates back on.

A week later, me and Ciaira were off to Milan. I found out quick that this fashion shit was not just about looking good but a ton of hard work. Ciaira was in her zone though. She loved that fashion shit like I loved moving weight. The same approach I took to running the dope game, my girl took to running the clothing game. About a week before the actual showcase, we went on a model search. Some of Ciaira contacts had put us in touch with a few agencies. The final one we went to, something about it just felt different when we walked through the door. Like it was my destiny to be there. I was already feeling kinda skittish because the night before I dreamed about Randi. I dreamed we were in a room together and we both were crying and there was blood on my hands. And the devil was standing in the corner smiling at us. Randi just kept saying please Keeli no. I woke up drenched in sweat and heart racing. I told Ciaira about my dream and she said it was the weed and me being semi paranoid that Juan may step out again. I would be lying if I said I wasn't because well he had already proven he was very capable of cheating. I smoked another blunt and went back to sleep and woke up feeling different. I can't really describe it but it was different.

So anyway, me and Ciaira are sitting in there agency checking out their portfolios of models and low and behold who do I come across but Ms. Randi herself. Everything started coming back to me about my dream and I was trying to put it together. Something about Randi showing up when she did unannounced and unexpected just always felt phony to me. So now I was about to start investigating. And the first part of my investigation was starting now with the receptionist chick Abby who had been checking me out, eating my pussy in her mind the whole time we had been in this piece."

Keeli stands up from her seat and starts to adjust her skirt that has rode up her thighs causing Abby to stare at them and smile. Keeli smiles at her and walks over to her desk. She sits down in the seat across from her and crosses her legs, exposing just enough thigh to make Abby subconsciously lick her lips.

"Hey Abby, remember you said if there was ANYTHING you could do to help make my time here more pleasurable, to just let you know." Keeli smiles seductively.
"Yes." Abby says with excitement, allowing her imagination to take flight. "Anything. Just name it."
Keeli opens the portfolio to Maranda's profile and shows the picture to Abby. "Her. I want you to tell me everything you know about her."
"Oh." Abby responds in a defeated tone. " I don't even know how that got in there. That should've been taken out. Randi hasn't worked with us in over three years."
"So there's nothing you can tell me about her?" I know her personally. She is a really close friend of my family. Our families are like family and we haven't heard from her in years. She's like a sister to me. Her daughter, Infinity I practically raised. But she just dropped off the face of the earth and we haven't heard from her and we all our worried." Keeli has a lone tear drop from her eye.
"Wow, I'm so sorry to hear that. I'll tell you what. This could cost me my job but for you, that's a risk I'm willing to take." Abby writes down an address on a piece of paper and hands it to Keeli. "This is one of my favorite restaurants. Meet me here this evening just for drinks and I may be able to provide you a lead or two."
Don't bullshit me Abby."
"I'm not. I promise it will be worth your while."
"Alright then. I will see you this evening."
"Eight is good."
"Cool."

"I went back over to Ciaira who was trying so hard to stifle a laugh and we left. She kept cracking jokes about the grand tongue lashing I was gonna get this evening. And while I had no attraction to women at all, I could pretend if that's what was needed to find out more about this home wrecking whore Randi who was tryna get me three hots and a cot.

We went back to the room and chilled out and then I got ready for the date I would never ever admit to having. I hoped in a cab and was on my way to the spot. Abby ass was already there and she looked good too. If I was sneaking over on the other side, Abby definitely would've been able to get it. We sat at the bar and had a couple drinks. Laughed and talked and shared a few appetizers. She was actually really good company. When the evening was over we walked outside and she hailed me a cab and gave me a paper with Randi's old roommate Epiphany's address and number on it. She shocked me when she leaned in and kissed me and you know what, I can't front. It was nice as fuck. I knew her head game had to be a monster from the way she kissed me. I felt my pussy get so wet and finally had to break away before I had an experimentation moment.

The next morning me and Ciaira went to

breakfast and then I asked her if she would be cool taking care of the business of the day on her own because I was gonna go holla at this Epiphany bitch. She said cool and we agreed to meet up for dinner that night. We both jumped in cabs heading in opposite directions to handle different aspect of business.

I was nervous as fuck heading to this broad house because I had no clue what the hell I was about to walk into. I mean I had her number and shit but decided not to call because the element of surprise is always way better. I just prayed I wasn't the one walking into a surprise and shit.

I got to the apartment and found out that nobody was home, but I was so pressed I couldn't just get on about my business like a normal person. I NEEDED to know more about this bitch. And my heart told me what I needed to know was inside the those walls. Lucky for me, the apartment ground floor and faced the rear. So I went around to what I took to be one of the bedroom windows, crawled through the bushes, used a nail file that was in my purse to cut the screen and WHAM! Just as I expected the window was unlocked because people just don't always remember to lock them bitches. I opened it up and slid right on inside.

I said a silent prayer that nobody was really home and then I peeked around a bit. Once I was sure I was alone, I got on my mission. In the living room I found a picture from a wedding, and Randi skank ass was staring as the bride. Her husband was fine as fuck, although I couldn't make out what his nationality was I knew he was fine and from the looks of that big ass wedding, his paper was loooong. I grabbed the picture and put in in my purse. Next I checked the bedroom that I figured used to be Randi's because there were a bunch of boxes packed up and unsealed that said "Randi's Stuff" I started going through them and aside from some old clothes, a few trinkets I didn't find much at first. Then I came upon a locked keepsake box at the bottom. It needed a key to be opened and I didn't have time to search for it. So I tucked the box under my arm and decided to get ghost. I had been in there for over an hour and felt like I was officially pushing my luck. I decided to head out the same way I got in, and I was glad that I did because by time I made it out and around to the front of the building, Epiphany, who I was able to identify from her pictures was hoping out of a cab with some shopping bags. I slid right in the cab she had gotten out of and was gone with the wind.

We rode across town in silence. The driver

kept peeking at me like what the fuck is really going on but he didn't dare ask and when I handed his ass double his fair, he just smiled and stop giving a fuck why I looked so suspect. And speaking of suspect, boy did I feel suspect as shit walking through the lobby of that expensive ass hotel we were staying in with dirt stains on my knees and a stolen box under my arm. I went upstairs, stripped naked, rolled a blunt and made me a drink from the bar. I used the heel of one of my shoes to crack the cheap lock on the box and then sat back ready to explore.

I found three letters addressed to Juan and TiTi but obviously she had never mailed. Six letters from him to her and two of them had never been opened. There was an invitation to Maranda and her husband Alexsander's wedding. There was also a copy of the marriage license and that was awesome for me because everything I needed to know about Mr and Mrs. Cumani was right in front of me for the most part, but I had to do a bit more digging first.

At the bottom of the box, I found a picture that sat my damn soul on fire. It was a picture of Juan, Randi and Ti on her first birthday. That picture had me hotter than fish grease. Why? Because they looked so fucking happy together and no, I couldn't *take it. I wanted that bitch to die so bad I could taste it. She was a thorn in my ass that needed to be pulled a long ass time ago.*

When I finished going through the box, I got on the internet and did some digging. By time I was done, I had Aleksander's telephone number and directions to his home if I wanted to go there. I opted to call him first, because judging from his demeanor in his wedding picture, he didn't seem like the type of dude you just popped up on askin questions and shit. So I called and was surprised at how polite he was. To my surprise, he was coming to Milan in two days for business and offered to meet with me then so we could discuss his estranged wife face to face and I was more than happy. Waiting two more days to find out this bitch real deal was gonna drive me insane but I knew I was gonna be worth my while.

I kept myself busy the next two days helping Ciaira get the final shit in place for the show. It was hard as hell to focus because my mind stayed on my upcoming meeting with Aleksander and that's all I really cared about. FINALLY, after what felt like 400 years, I got the call I had been waiting for from Randi's husband. We agreed to meet at a restaurant that was midway between our hotels, ironically, it was right next to the place Abby had taken me. I left Ciaira at the venue filling out last minute paper work and went back to the hotel to get ready. I showered, flat ironed my hair and slipped into an all white Versace sundress and matching gladiator sandals. I even went as far as to throw on the a white oversized sunhat and a white Versace bag and was out the door. I hopped in a cab and was on the way to find out what I was destined to find out on this trip. Exactly why Randi stanking ass was in my country breathing my air and making my life fucking hell.

When I walked into the restaurant, I was immediately pulled in by the smell of the food. Simply amazing. The atmosphere was nice also. I gave the hostess my name and she showed me to the table where Aleksander was already seated. His Albanian ass was cuter than his picture but he was no Juan. Still fine as a motherfucka tho. He stood up to greet me and I couldn't help but smile. I had to admit, although I hated Maranda's stankin ass, she had amazing taste in men. His big face rolex, tailored suit and Versace shoes greeted me before he could. He was a complete gentlemen as he pulled out my chair for me and ordered us wine and poured my glass. He seemed like an amazing man and I couldn't understand why Maranda was running from him. I hated pussyfooting around and apparently he did too because before I could think of a way to approach the situation at hand without sounding so crass, he came out with it.

"So Keeli, please tell me. Why the interest in my wife?" Aleksander ask with a heavy Albanian accent.
"You don't waste any time huh." Keeli chuckles.
"No point in prolonging the inevitable."
"You have a point there."
"So again, tell me. Why they interest in my wife?"
"Okay, I wasn't completely honest with you during our phone conversation. Me and Maranda are not old friends."
"I am not surprised."
"Well I am married to her ex. Her daughter's father."
"I'm sorry, I think there has been some confusion. Maranda only has one child. Our son Micah."
"I beg to differ." Keeli says as she goes into her purse and pulls out the picture of Juan, Randi and Ti that she took from the box. She slides it over to Aleksander. He looks at it and shakes his head in disgust. "This slut and her lies just doesn't end."
"I came to you because this bitch has been a pain in my ass since the day she showed up at my house. She claimed she missed her daughter so much that she gave up modeling to move back to the states.
"Maranda gave up modeling a long time ago."
"I know that now."

"So how long has she been in the states?" Aleksander asks, now completely invested in his meeting with Keeli. "Since last August. And she never once mentioned the family she left behind. She has just been focusing on ruining mine and now I may go to jail because of her. Please, just tell me why she left." Keeli pleads, as angry tears begin to fill her eyes as the memory of all the hurt she experienced due to Juan's affair with Maranda comes rushing back.

Aleksander wipes Keeli's eyes with a cloth napkin. "I usually don't discuss other people's business. But I can see the pain Maranda's presence has brought you is great. Maranda got mixed up with the wrong people. Her and her accomplice stole close to 300 million dollars from what turned out to be the wrong person. Her accomplice was killed, and she somehow managed to slip out of the country undetected."

Keeli is sitting there with her mouth hanging open in utter shock at Maranda's real deal. "Did she get away with the money?"

"Not exactly. The money is in a Swiss account that has a double password protection order on it. So with her accomplice gone, she can't touch it because he didn't trust her enough to give her the second password. So now she is broke and wanted so she can't come home because they will kill her the minute she steps off a plane."

"Wow. This shit is unbelievable. And so they haven't come after you and Micah?

"No. They are not the kind to harm innocent people. They only want her and I'm certain they wont stop until they get her.

"Damn."

"I really didn't even know what else to say. This was not the shit I was expecting to

hear when I sat down at the table with Aleksander. I always said it was more to her surprise arrival. I just never knew or expected it to be this much. Shit was officially crazy.

Me and Aleksander ate, drank and talked, but no more about Maranda. Just about stuff. Half of it I don't even remember because I couldn't take my mind off the fact that Maranda was in shit that was way too deep to dig out of. Once dinner was over, Aleksander paid, brought me roses and hailed me a cab. I thanked him for meeting with me again and he gave me a picture of him, Maranda and their son Micah who was adorable, He looked just like Ti in a lot of aspects. He asked me to give the picture to Maranda and just ask her was it worth it.

Riding back to the hotel, I felt so bad for Aleksander. He really seemed like a good dude. And because Again, I had said it from day one that the bitch was suspect and now I was so glad I had the evidence to prove it. I couldn't wait to get home. I was giving this bitch 2 options the moment I touched down.

1)Drop the charges for starters and get the fuck outta my town FOREVER. Or
2)I expose her to Juan for starters and if he didn't put a bullet in that bitch head

for lying to him, it was nothing for me to reach out to Aleksander again and find out where these wrong peoples were at and let them know where she said her prayers at nightly.

The bitch was smart enough to halfway steal 300 million dollars, I was positive she would go with option 1.

The next few days I kept myself busy helping Ciaira get shit in gear for the show and I found out that fashion was hard work. I was so over that shit by time them bitches hit the runway it aint make no sense, but Ciaira. That chick was right at home, She ran that fashion set like I ran the streets. HARD AS FUCK. I was proud as shit seeing my girl living out her dreams and prouder to know that it was my plan that made all this shit possible.

After the fashion show was over and our line KILLED IT, We went to a star studded after party with some of the biggest names period. Kimora Lee Simmons and Russell were in the building. Oprah fucking Winfrey was in the building. And truth be told nobody else fucking mattered. We were in the same venue as Oprah. Life was officially being lived. After we hob nobbed for a spell or two we went back to our hotel and finally got some real sleep. We had been running

since our plane landed because Ciaira was determined not a stitch was gonna be outta place and it wasn't. I slept like a baby and woke up feeling like I was gonna bust if I didn't get home and handle my business IMMEDIATELY. So we agreed to cut our trip short and flew home the following day.

It was 3 days before Me and Juan's Anniversary when we got home and I was so excited. When I pulled up in our driveway, I barely had the car in park when I jumped out and sprinted for the house. I wanted to hug and kiss my family and just be in their presence. While I was on the plane I thought I wanted my first stop to be Randi's house but the closer I got to America, the faster my thoughts of Randi were replaced with my husband and kids. And by time our plane taxied in, I just wanted to be with the people I loved. So she had a few more days to walk around with her secrets and shit.

On our Anniversary, Juan surprised me with a huge Anniversary party at our house and I loved it. We didn't too much trip off of gifts because well what do you really get the person who has everything and all they don't got they don't want? So we just chilled with the family and enjoyed our party . I spent the next week home with my family doing nothing at all but enjoying my family and fucking my husband like I was his mistress. But the following week, it was time to get back to business on all fronts.

My kids started summer camp so I had my days free to work and get shit done. I just to be safe. I still wasn't touching the work or really going on the same side of town as that shit just to be safe. Ty had been running shit just fine and as my Grandma Wanda always would say "If the shit aint broke, don't fuck with it." So I didn't. Ty was showing me what he was made of at this point. My money was always straight down to the penny and ON TIME. He kept the crews in check and made sure when motherfuckas hit that block they was on the grind. Wasn't no time to play. He made sure the clientele was getting their shit on time and everything. I almost felt like the nigga was vying for my spot the way he was working shit. But seriously, I expected nothing less from my nigga.

Since my crew wasn't working Isherwood no more, I hadn't had any more issues with Jake B, but we still needed a sit down because that block was a cash cow and since my peoples had paid their debts, I was planning to let that motherfucka graze sooner rather than later.

On Monday morning me and the brats dropped Juan off at the airport. Him and Roc were going to check out some properties in Utah that had landed on their radar. Once they boarded the plane safely, I dropped the boys off at martial arts camp and Asha at dance camp. From there I had to orders of business to handle before I met CiCi at my mother's house for our lunch date.

My first stop was to see good ole Randi. I was smiling all the way there because I knew once I said what I needed to say, the bitch would be so shook her ass was gonna be on the next thing smoking out of my neck of the woods. I wanted that bitch a long ass way from DC before Juan got back on Wednesday. She lived in a big shit High Rise in upper North West. The National Cathedral was literally in this broad back yard. And now since I knew she was 100% broke because she couldn't get her hands on that stolen money she had across the ocean I was sure Juan had been eating this bitch bills the whole time behind my back. But it was all good cause that shit was stopping as of TODAY.

I parked across the street from her fancy ass building and strolled right on in. Now as hefty as the ticket was to live in this neck of the woods, it was amazing that the front desk clerk was off on a cigarette break or some shit cause he or she definitely wasn't keeping the building rid of bitches with big ass guns in their purse like I. So I strolled on to the elevator and made my way to the 6th floor, found unit 673 and rang the peep-hole-less doorbell. A minute later, Randi opened the door and damn near shit herself when she saw it was me. Bitch looked as scared as a long tailed cat in a room full of rocking chairs.

I couldn't help but laugh when she called herself trying to close the door back on me, but I wasn't leaving until I made sure that bitch UNDERSTOOD she was no longer welcome in the Nation's Capital. Fuck, her ass was no longer welcome on the same continent as me. So I stuck my foot in the door and me and her had a stare off for all of 60 seconds, then she finally gave up and fell back. So I pushed her little stupid ass door open and strolled up in that bitch like I was Queen of the motherfucking UNIVERSE. She was shook, but I guess she figured she would take her chances with me inside her house than dealing with what may pop off if the bitch said it with her motherfuckin chest. I strolled over to her bar like it was mine and sat down and made myself a drink. She stood there shook as shit not knowing how to take the scene unfolding before her. I could hear that bitch heart thump with her scared ass. I sat there mixing my drink and enjoying every moment of this bitch being shook. I think my silence scared her ass *more than my presence. I let her stew in her fear for a whole 10 minutes. She literally just stood there by the door looking scared as shit in her own house. It finally got boring watching this bitch make peace with Jesus silently because she KNEW I was there to take her life. So I finally decided to get down to business. I walked over to her sitting area and took a seat."*

"I didn't come to lay hands on you this time. I just need to talk to you." Keeli says and sips her drink.

"Look Keeli, Juan and I are not seeing each other anymore if that's what you think. I left him alone so we don't have anything to talk about." Maranda says on the verge of tears.

"Oh I beg to differ." Keeli smiles as she goes in her bag and pulls out her 9mm beretta and lays in on her lap. She goes back in the bag and pulls out the picture Aleksander had given her and lays it on the glass coffee table. Randi looks at the picture and her eyes well up with tears and they start to fall without her consent. "So do you want to talk now?" Keeli asks and finishes off her drink.

Randi walks over slowly and picks up the picture and stares at it silently for almost two minutes before she wipes her eyes and speaks. "Where did you get this photo from?"

"I think you know where I got it from Randi. Me and Aleksander had a very informative meeting while I was in Milan. He told me everything darling."

"Everything about what?" Randi asks, feeling somewhere between angry and scared.

"Don't fucking play with me Randi. He told me about the 300 million fucking dollars you stole for starters dumb

ass. He told me about the Swiss account that your ass
can't access. I know about your accomplice being killed
and you calling yourself going on the lamb. Well it looks
like you pick the wrong place to get off that bitch huh."
Keeli laughs at Randi's agony.
Randi sits on the plush sofa across from Keeli to steady
herself and starts to cry uncontrollably. She sobs through
her tears. "That's not how it happened at all. That wasn't
Aleksander you met Keeli. Aleksander is dead. That was
his twin brother Armend. I didn't steal anything, Armend
..."
"Look! I don't care. I don't give a fuck who stole what or
who the fuck shot John. All I want you to do is drop the
fucking charges against me, pack your shit and get the
fuck off my side of the earth.
"What? Maranda asked, completely confused.
"Oh bitch you heard me. You got 60 days to drop them
charges, pack your shit and get the fuck gone. Don't
leave no forwarding number or no forwarding address.
You just get the fuck on cause if you don't I got a direct
line to Aleksander, Armend or whoever the fuck he is and
I will most certainly call him and tell him where to find
your scheming shiesty ass at.
"What about Ti?"
"What about her? She gonna bring her ass home with me
and her father where she belongs and if you ever contact
ANYBODY who has the same last name as me again ole
boy aint gonna be your problem." You got me?." Randi
nods her head yes as the tears continue to fall from her
eyes. Keeli sticks the picture and her gun back in her
purse then gets up and walks to the door. "You got 60
days Maranda. 60 days." Keeli walks out and closes the
door behind her.

*"That went pretty well of you ask me. I
really didn't want to be the person to make
Ti stand over her mother in a coffin while I*

consoled her little ass BUT if her mammy aint heed my warning I was gonna lay her ass down with no further discussion THEN ride in the family car to her fucking services."

"CONFESSIONS"

"Now that I had taken care of this Randi shit, my next order of business was to get with Daye because it was time for a meet with the motherfucking boogie man. I drove to the rec center because I knew that was his spot and sure enough he was there. This time I didn't even have to waste verbiage on his yes men because they KNEW BETTER than to say shit to me outside of "Hello" and "Let me go get him." After they got him, me and him went up to his office to discuss the situation at hand."

Keeli sits down in the chair across from Daye and takes a deep breath. "Daye, there is a serious fucking problem."
"Tell me about it yo." Daye sympathizes with Keeli. "That's fucked up what happened to your peoples. I thought you would've been came to holla at me yo."
"I would've but I had some other shit to deal with on a personal level. But yo, I need a meeting with your man."
"Who? B?"
"Yes. I thought this whole shit was squashed between us."
"It is between me and you. You already know that baby girl. I tried to talk to dude about what he doing but he aint tryna hear me. He was on some ole pulling rank shit and all."
"Look, I need you to set that meeting up. Whatever it takes."
"Alright. I'ma try and talk to him again. I aint promising nothing but I will try for you. Get with me next week and I'll let you know what's up."
"Alright Daye." Keeli stands up and her and Daye exchange a hug and then she leaves.

"After I left the meet with Daye, I went straight to my mother's house and picked up CiCi, Adovia and Sy. We rode out to Potomac Mills and did some shopping and then had a late lunch. While we rode out, CiCi put me down on how shit was going on his side of town. His aunt and cousin was doing super bad from what he was telling me. He said if I saw Tiff, I wouldn't even recognize her cause she was so fucked up on that shit these days. He also told me that Jackie and Simm had fell out recently. He said they had words about me. Apparently Jackie still felt some kinda way about Simm taking advantage of me when he went to jail. And in a way I agreed with Jackie. That nigga saw how desolate my situation was and used that as his way to push up on me. So they wasn't beefing but they aint have shit to say to each other these days. While a part of me appreciated Jackie caring enough about me to be mad all these years later, there was that other part of me that felt like this nigga aint need to go losing no friends on my account. I had long ago made my peace with Simm in my head and heart and as long as he stayed the fuck out of my line of vision, he could live. So Jackie ass aint have to go be no Martyr for me. I was good on all that shit.

On Wednesday night, Juan got home and shit was just as it has been between us since we reconciled.   I wasn't at all worried about Randi ringing him up and telling him about my little visit because if she did she would have to explain Aleksander and the stolen money and all that shit to him. And besides, I would kill her for real and she knew it.

The following week I was able to squeeze in a few minutes to get with Daye. I showed up expecting to get a time and place for the meet with Jake B. Instead all I got was his word that I was a dead woman walking. Daye said dude was like "Fuck her, I aint meeting that bitch. And my peoples aint gonna stop bussin their guns until her whole fucking FAMILY both blood and brought is dead. POINT BLANK"

Now I done kept it 100 with you since you've been reading this shit, so for me to say anything at this point other than I WAS SCARED would be me not keeping it 100 point blank. So yes, hearing this nigga wanted me and anybody who ever smiled in my fucking direction dead scared me. I had heard all the horror stories on this nigga and from the way the streets told it, his bullets aint stop for women and children. So knowing this fucking psychopath wanted me and all four of mine dead had me feeling quite shook. When I left Daye I had made up my mind what I needed to do. I had to stop playing around and tell Juan what was going on out here in these streets. It was past time for me to put him on to this shit And that night I made it my business to do just that."

Juan is laying on the bed watching TV. Keeli comes in the room in her pajamas and closes the door. She walks over to the bed and gets under the over and snuggles up to Juan. He leans down and kisses her on her forehead.
"Her little ass finally went to sleep huh.?"
"Yes." Keeli responds dryly before reaching over and grabbing the remote and turning the TV off.
"Yo what you do that for? I was watching that baby."
"We gotta talk Juan. And it's serious."
"Alright." Juan sits up straight and leans against the headboard. "What's up?"
"Papi, I kinda got myself in a pickle."
"What's going on now Keeli?" Juan asks in an exhausted tone.
"Alright so a few months ago, like back in January actually, A beef started up. Well it actually started up when them two dopefiend bitches did some stupid shit and..."
"Stop talking in circles Keeli and get to the point." Juan snaps, already annoyed with the conversation.
"Alright. So this guy name Jake B wants to dead me and my whole crew over some shit Tiff and CoCo pulled. His peoples already hit one of my spots and killed three of me people and..."
"What the fuck! When did this happen?"

"Back in January."

"And why the fuck is you just now telling me!"

"I don't know! Shit was already strained between us. Plus I thought I could handle it. But now this nigga talking about killing me and everybody I know and from what I hear he aint no joke." Keeli says just as tears start to fall from her eyes.

"Keeli listen...."

"Baby I'm scared." Keeli confesses. "The whole time I been in this shit, any beef or situation that came my way I stood tall and handled that shit. I aint got no issues with bussin my gun..."

"Keeli..." Juan attempts to interrupt her speech.

"But baby, it's hard as fuck to put a beam on your enemy when you don't even know how to find the motherfucka or what he looks like."

Juan chuckles at Keeli's revelation. "So wait a minute, you aint never seen Jake B before?"

"No." Keeli confesses. It's just his name and his rep stay floating in the streets. But I aint never laid eyes on the nigga before."

"So wait a minute. If you aint never even seen this nigga before, how you know he talking about killing you and shit."

"Daye put me on to how this nigga feeling. When the shit first came about, I went to him to find out what was up . All this shit is because of Tiff and CoCo. They went at him and had his fucking daughter killed."

"His daughter?" Juan asked, now confused.

"Yes. His daughter."

Juan gets a worried look on his face. "Well mami, I don't really know what to say. I've heard about the nigga too and how he get down."

"So now you know why I'm scared."

"I aint say all that." Juan gets out of the bed. "Just try and get some sleep and..."

"I can't..." Keeli begins to protest.

"Just do what I said! I'll be back!" Juan heads towards

the door.

"Wait! Where are you going?"

"Since you done managed to pull us into a fucking war with motherfucking terrorist, I gotta make sure we ready before we all fucking end up dead! Now you see why the fuck I told you to stay out of this shit! But you fucking hard headed." Juan walks out the bedroom and slams the door.

"Seeing Juan and how he was looking aint really do much to calm my fears. I aint never known Papi or nobody he fucked with to hold fear in their hearts, but I was wondering if we would make it outta this war ok. All I knew was if one of my kids died behind some shit Tiff and CoCo did and more than likely Simm put their asses up to the shit I promised to God I was gonna kill everybody who ever held them motherfuckas closes. I was also now looking at Jackie's ass differently and worried about his role in this shit. I made a mental note to hit him up in the morning for a meet because I needed to know everything that went down and who pulled the strings cause they definitely had to go. If I had to do my own sister and cousin behind this shit, then so be it. They had literally fucked with the wrong nigga and now too many other people were paying for that shit.

I laid there unable to sleep and then the million dollar question crossed my mind. If I had it all to do over again, would I have chosen the same roads? And truth be told, I probably wouldn't.   Don't get me wrong, I was thankful for every dollar I had made in these streets. I was thankful to be able to provide for my family like never before ...

BUT...

None of this shit was worth dying for or worse, having one of my kids or my husband die behind. But it was far too late for if's and buts. We all know that saying. "If If's and Buts were candy and nuts we'd all be 900 pounds with fucked up teeth. So now I had to suck it up and deal with it.

Now true enough if they did get at us and the blood of my husband, one of our children or myself happened to spill. Nobody Jake B knew would be safe on the planet earth. Motherfuckas would have to move to mars asap. But that still wouldn't bring the dead back so I was praying that by now involving Papi, we would be able to get at them before they could get at us."

Queen Of DC 3: The Story Of My Demise.   K Sherrie

"Am I my Spouse's Keeper?"

"I finally managed to fall asleep close to 5am. I woke up a little after 10 and was beyond pissed off. I overslept so that meant I would be stuck with my kids all day and while I loved their asses with all that I was, my mind was cluttered with this Jake B shit so I had no more patience left to deal with the bullshit of my clan. I threw on my robe and made my way downstairs and my house was quiet. Too quiet. I didn't understand that because my kids rose with the sun and when them motherfuckas was up, they let you KNOW their asses was up. I walked around for a minute and finally found Papi in the kitchen. He was sitting at the table reading the newspaper and eating a bowl of fruit loops. I didn't understand how the fuck he could be some calm, like we all weren't scheduled to die as early as today!"

Juan smiles at Keeli when he sees her standing in there watching him. "Good morning."
"What's up. Where the kids at?"
"At camp. I dropped them off. Why don't you grab something to eat? You barely touched your dinner last night."
"Nah I'm good. Eating is like the furthest thing from my mind right now."
"Suit yourself." Juan says as he continues to eat his breakfast.
"Baby..." Keeli starts to express her thoughts. "Baby I was thinking, maybe we should just take the kids and move down to Panama for a while and..."

"What?" Juan asks in disbelief.

"I'm serious. Let's just take the kids and just go. I'll sell my business, QDC will be the first to go. Fuck I'll give them shits away. Let's just go please."

Juan looks at Keeli and takes in the look of fear on her face. He lets out an exhausted sigh. "Ke, is you really that scared?"

"Yes! This nigga that neither of us have ever laid eyes on wants to kill us and our kids. I can't let that shit happen!"

"Ke calm down. You getting yourself all worked up."

"This nigga threatened our fucking family Juan! How the fuck am I NOT supposed to be worked up!" Keeli snaps as she starts to cry.

"That's not what I'm saying. Look, go take a shower and get dressed. I want you to come take a ride with me."

"Take a ride with you... The fuck you think this nigga playing Juan?!"

Juan jumps up and smacks the bowl of cereal he was eating off the table. "Shut the fuck up and just do it! Remember it was your simple hardheaded ass that go us the fuck in this shit in the first place!"

Keeli walks out the kitchen without saying another word for two reasons. Knowing that Juan was right and not knowing where her protesting taking a ride would take things between them. Once she gets dressed, Her and Juan drive out to Newington Virginia. Juan drives onto the huge farm property with a newly built single family estate sitting in the middle of it. Juan drives up the long driveway and stops in front of the oversized double doors. He turns the truck off and looks over at Keeli. "Come on."

"Who's house is this Juan?"

"Man just come the fuck on." Juan gets out of his Range Rover and Keeli follows suit. They walk up to the double doors without saying another word to each other. Juan rings the doorbell and waits. A minute later a man a little over 6 feet tall with skin the color of dark chocolate, green eyes and dreads that hang down the middle of his

back opens the door. He smiles at Juan and the two men exchange a familiar hug. He finally speaks in a thick Jamaican accent. "Good ta see ya boy. I thought ya wasn't coming for a second dere. Come on in." The man steps to the side and allows Juan and Keeli to enter the house before closing the door. He leads them down the foyer and into the huge sunken living room. The 3 of them take seat on the oversized custom sectional. The man picks up a blunt from the ashtray on the glass table and sparks it. He takes a deep pull and then passes it to Juan. "So what brings ya way out here to see me?"
"Oh yeah, let me introduce y'all before we get to that. Unc, this is my wife Keeli. And babe this is my uncle. His name is Bobby, but the streets call him Jake B."

Available now from the pen of K Sherrie:

Queen Of DC 4: The Book of Revelations

CPSIA information can be obtained
at www.ICGtesting.com
Printed in the USA
BVHW030026230321
603191BV00004B/113